O. Henry
The Four Million

SELECTED STORIES
Large Print

D1736677

América en Libros

SAN JUAN, PUERTO RICO

For information contact:
América en Libros
info@americaenlibros.com

First Edition
Print, March 2021

Table of Contents

Biographical Note

O. Henry
Pen name of William Sydney Porter
(Greensboro, NC, 11 September 1862 – New York City, 5 June 1910)

Writer of several hundred short stories that are characterized for their surprising endings. As a young man he clerked in his uncle's drugstore and was licensed as a pharmacist. When he was 20 he went to Texas, where he eventually worked as teller in the First National Bank in Austin. He began writing sketches at about the time of his marriage to Athol Estes in 1887 and later started weekly, The Rolling Stone. When that venture failed, he joined the Houston Post. In February 1896 he was indicted for embezzlement and he fled to Honduras, where he lived for several months. There he wrote *Cabbages and Kings* and is credited with coining the term "banana republic." He returned to the U.S. when his wife was gravely ill. After her death he entered the penitentiary at Columbus, Ohio. During his sentence he worked as night druggist in the prison hospital, where he could write. During this time he used various pseudonyms but became best known as O. Henry. In 1902 he arrived in New York, and for a few years wrote a story a week for the *New York Sunday World* in addition to writing for other magazines. He was a heavy drinker and in his final years his ill health affected his writing. The O. Henry Prize, given annually to outstanding short stories, was established in his honor in 1919.

Other Books from América en Libros

O. Henry Selected Stories in Large Print

The Four Million, Selected Stories
The Trimmed Lamp and other Stories of the Four Million, Selected Stories
The Voice of the City: Further Stories of the Four Million, Selected Stories
Strictly Business: More Stories of the Four Million, Selected Stories

O. Henry The Four Million Word Search in Large Print

The Four Million Word Search Volume 1 Large Print
The Four Million Word Search Volume 2 Large Print
The Four Million Word Search Volume 3 Large Print
The Four Million Word Search Volume 4 Large Print

Bible Word Search Pentateuch in Large Print

Bible Word Search Pentateuch Volume 1 Large Print
Bible Word Search Pentateuch Volume 2 Large Print
Bible Word Search Pentateuch Anthology 1 Large Print

Bible Word Search Historical Books in Large Print

Bible Word Search Historical Books Volume 1 Large Print

Selected Stories

Note on the Selected Stories

The 20 selected short stories in this volume were originally part of the 25 stories published in 1906 in *The Four Million*. The stories are not presented in the order of original publication.

The five stories published in *The Four Million* and not selected for publication in this anthology are:

An Adjustment of Nature
Sisters of The Golden Circle
The Caliph, Cupid and the Clock
The Green Door
Tobin's Palm

BY COURIER

It was neither the season nor the hour when the Park had frequenters; and it is likely that the young lady, who was seated on one of the benches at the side of the walk, had merely obeyed a sudden impulse to sit for a while and enjoy a foretaste of coming Spring.

She rested there, pensive and still. A certain melancholy that touched her countenance must have been of recent birth, for it had not yet altered the fine and youthful contours of her cheek, nor subdued the arch though resolute curve of her lips.

A tall young man came striding through the park along the path near which she sat. Behind him tagged a boy carrying a suit-case. At sight of the young lady, the man's face changed to red and back to pale again. He watched her countenance as he drew nearer, with hope and anxiety mingled on his own. He passed within a few yards of her, but he saw no evidence that she was aware of his presence or existence.

Some fifty yards further on he suddenly stopped and sat on a bench at one side. The boy dropped the suit-case and stared at him with wondering, shrewd eyes. The young man took out his handkerchief and wiped his brow. It was a good handkerchief, a good brow, and the young man was good to look at. He said to the boy:

"I want you to take a message to that young lady on that bench. Tell her I am on my way to the station, to leave for San Francisco, where I shall join that Alaska moose-hunting expedition. Tell her that, since she has commanded me neither to speak nor to write to her, I take this means of making one last appeal to her sense of justice, for the sake of what has been. Tell her that to condemn and discard one who has not deserved such treatment, without giving him her reasons or a chance to explain is contrary to her nature as I believe it to be. Tell her that I have thus, to a certain degree, disobeyed her injunctions, in the hope that she may yet be inclined to see justice done. Go, and tell her that."

The young man dropped a half-dollar into the boy's hand. The boy looked at him for a moment with bright, canny eyes out of a dirty, intelligent face, and then set off at a run. He approached the lady on the bench a little doubtfully, but unembarrassed. He touched the brim of the old plaid bicycle cap perched on the back of his head. The lady looked at him coolly, without prejudice or favour.

"Lady," he said, "dat gent on de oder bench sent yer a song and dance by me. If yer don't know de guy, and he's tryin' to do de Johnny act, say de word, and I'll call a cop in t'ree minutes. If yer does know him, and he's on de square, w'y I'll spiel yer de bunch of hot air he sent yer."

The young lady betrayed a faint interest.

"A song and dance!" she said, in a deliberate sweet voice that seemed to clothe her words in a diaphanous garment of impalpable irony. "A new idea—in the troubadour line, I suppose. I—used to know the gentleman who sent you, so I think it will hardly be necessary to call the police. You may execute your song and dance, but do not sing too loudly. It is a little early yet for open-air vaudeville, and we might attract attention."

"Awe," said the boy, with a shrug down the length of him, "yer know what I mean, lady. 'Tain't a turn, it's wind. He told me to tell yer he's got his collars and cuffs in dat grip for a scoot clean out to 'Frisco. Den he's goin' to shoot snow-birds in de Klondike. He says yer told him not to send 'round no more pink notes nor come hangin' over de garden gate, and he takes dis means of puttin' yer wise. He says yer refereed him out like a has-been, and never give him no chance to kick at de decision. He says yer swiped him, and never said why."

The slightly awakened interest in the young lady's eyes did not abate. Perhaps it was caused by either the originality or the audacity of the snow-bird hunter, in thus circumventing her express commands against the ordinary modes of communication. She fixed her eye on a statue standing disconsolate in the dishevelled park, and spoke into the transmitter:

"Tell the gentleman that I need not repeat to him a description of my ideals. He knows what they have been and what they still are. So far as they touch on this case, absolute loyalty and truth are the ones paramount. Tell him that I have studied my own heart as well as one can, and I know its weakness as well as I do its needs. That is why I decline to hear his pleas, whatever they may be. I did not condemn him through hearsay or doubtful evidence, and that is why I made no charge. But, since he persists in hearing what he already well knows, you may convey the matter.

"Tell him that I entered the conservatory that evening from the rear, to cut a rose for my mother. Tell him I saw him and Miss Ashburton beneath the pink oleander. The tableau was pretty, but the pose and juxtaposition were too eloquent and evident to require explanation. I left the conservatory, and, at the same time, the rose and my ideal. You may carry that song and dance to your impresario."

"I'm shy on one word, lady. Jux—jux—put me wise on dat, will yer?"

"Juxtaposition—or you may call it propinquity—or, if you like, being rather too near for one maintaining the position of an ideal."

The gravel spun from beneath the boy's feet. He stood by the other bench. The man's eyes interrogated him, hungrily. The boy's were shining with the impersonal zeal of the translator.

"De lady says dat she's on to de fact dat gals is dead easy when a feller comes spielin' ghost stories and tryin' to make up, and dat's why she won't listen to no soft-soap. She says she caught yer dead to rights, huggin' a bunch o' calico in de hot-house. She side-stepped in to pull some posies and yer was squeezin' de oder gal to beat de band. She says it looked cute, all right all right, but it made her sick. She says yer better git busy, and make a sneak for de train."

The young man gave a low whistle and his eyes flashed with a sudden thought. His hand flew to the inside pocket of his coat, and drew out a handful of letters. Selecting one, he handed it to the boy, following it with a silver dollar from his vest-pocket.

"Give that letter to the lady," he said, "and ask her to read it. Tell her that it should explain the situation. Tell her that, if she had mingled a little trust with her conception of the ideal, much heartache might have been avoided. Tell her that the loyalty she prizes so much has never wavered. Tell her I am waiting for an answer."

The messenger stood before the lady.

"De gent says he's had de ski-bunk put on him widout no cause. He says he's no bum guy; and, lady, yer read dat letter, and I'll bet yer he's a white sport, all right."

The young lady unfolded the letter; somewhat doubtfully, and read it.

> Dear Dr. Arnold: I want to thank you for your most kind and opportune aid to my daughter last Friday evening, when she was overcome by an attack of her old heart-trouble in the conservatory at Mrs. Waldron's reception. Had you not been near to catch her as she fell and to render proper attention, we might have lost her. I would be glad if you would call and undertake the treatment of her case.
>
> Gratefully yours,
>
> Robert Ashburton.

The young lady refolded the letter, and handed it to the boy.

"De gent wants an answer," said the messenger. "Wot's de word?"

The lady's eyes suddenly flashed on him, bright, smiling and wet.

"Tell that guy on the other bench," she said, with a happy, tremulous laugh, "that his girl wants him."

THE FURNISHED ROOM

Restless, shifting, fugacious as time itself is a certain vast bulk of the population of the red brick district of the lower West Side. Homeless, they have a hundred homes. They flit from furnished room to furnished room, transients forever—transients in abode, transients in heart and mind. They sing "Home, Sweet Home" in ragtime; they carry their lares et penates in a bandbox; their vine is entwined about a picture hat; a rubber plant is their fig tree.

Hence the houses of this district, having had a thousand dwellers, should have a thousand tales to tell, mostly dull ones, no doubt; but it would be strange if there could not be found a ghost or two in the wake of all these vagrant guests.

One evening after dark a young man prowled among these crumbling red mansions, ringing their bells. At the twelfth he rested his lean hand-baggage upon the step and wiped the dust from his hatband and forehead. The bell sounded faint and far away in some remote, hollow depths.

To the door of this, the twelfth house whose bell he had rung, came a housekeeper who made him think of an unwholesome, surfeited worm that had eaten its nut to a hollow shell and now sought to fill the vacancy with edible lodgers.

He asked if there was a room to let.

"Come in," said the housekeeper. Her voice came from her throat; her throat seemed lined with fur. "I have the third floor back, vacant since a week back. Should you wish to look at it?"

The young man followed her up the stairs. A faint light from no particular source mitigated the shadows of the halls. They trod noiselessly upon a stair carpet that its own loom would have forsworn. It seemed to have become vegetable; to have degenerated in that rank, sunless air to lush lichen or spreading moss that grew in patches to the staircase and was viscid under the foot like organic matter. At each turn of the stairs were vacant niches in the wall. Perhaps plants had once been set within them. If so they had died in that foul and tainted air. It may be that statues of the saints had stood there, but it was not difficult to conceive that imps and devils had dragged them forth in the darkness and down to the unholy depths of some furnished pit below.

"This is the room," said the housekeeper, from her furry throat. "It's a nice room. It ain't often vacant. I had some most elegant people in it last summer—no trouble at all, and paid in advance to the minute. The water's at the end of the hall. Sprowls and Mooney kept it three months. They done a vaudeville sketch. Miss B'retta Sprowls—you may have heard of her—Oh, that was just the stage names—right there over the dresser is where the marriage certificate hung, framed. The gas is here, and you see there is plenty of closet room. It's a room everybody likes. It never stays idle long."

"Do you have many theatrical people rooming here?" asked the young man.

"They comes and goes. A good proportion of my lodgers is connected with the theatres. Yes, sir, this is the theatrical district. Actor people never stays long anywhere. I get my share. Yes, they comes and they goes."

He engaged the room, paying for a week in advance. He was tired, he said, and would take possession at once. He counted out the money. The room had been made ready, she said, even to towels and water. As the housekeeper moved away he put, for the thousandth time, the question that he carried at the end of his tongue.

"A young girl—Miss Vashner—Miss Eloise Vashner—do you remember such a one among your lodgers? She would be singing on the stage, most likely. A fair girl, of medium height and slender, with reddish, gold hair and a dark mole near her left eyebrow."

"No, I don't remember the name. Them stage people has names they change as often as their rooms. They comes and they goes. No, I don't call that one to mind."

No. Always no. Five months of ceaseless interrogation and the inevitable negative. So much time spent by day in questioning managers, agents, schools and choruses; by night among the audiences of theatres from all-star casts down to music halls so low that he dreaded to find what he most hoped for. He who had loved her best had tried to find her. He was sure that since her disappearance from home this great, water-girt city held her somewhere, but it was

16

like a monstrous quicksand, shifting its particles constantly, with no foundation, its upper granules of to-day buried to-morrow in ooze and slime.

The furnished room received its latest guest with a first glow of pseudo-hospitality, a hectic, haggard, perfunctory welcome like the specious smile of a demirep. The sophistical comfort came in reflected gleams from the decayed furniture, the ragged brocade upholstery of a couch and two chairs, a foot-wide cheap pier glass between the two windows, from one or two gilt picture frames and a brass bedstead in a corner.

The guest reclined, inert, upon a chair, while the room, confused in speech as though it were an apartment in Babel, tried to discourse to him of its divers tenantry.

A polychromatic rug like some brilliant-flowered rectangular, tropical islet lay surrounded by a billowy sea of soiled matting. Upon the gay-papered wall were those pictures that pursue the homeless one from house to house—The Huguenot Lovers, The First Quarrel, The Wedding Breakfast, Psyche at the Fountain. The mantel's chastely severe outline was ingloriously veiled behind some pert drapery drawn rakishly askew like the sashes of the Amazonian ballet. Upon it was some desolate flotsam cast aside by the room's marooned when a lucky sail had borne them to a fresh port—a trifling vase or two, pictures of actresses, a medicine bottle, some stray cards out of a deck.

One by one, as the characters of a cryptograph become explicit, the little signs left by the furnished room's procession of guests developed a significance. The threadbare space in the rug in front of the dresser told that lovely woman had marched in the throng. Tiny finger prints on the wall spoke of little prisoners trying to feel their way to sun and air. A splattered stain, raying like the shadow of a bursting bomb, witnessed where a hurled glass or bottle had splintered with its contents against the wall. Across the pier glass had been scrawled with a diamond in staggering letters the name "Marie." It seemed that the succession of dwellers in the furnished room had turned in fury— perhaps tempted beyond forbearance by its garish coldness—and wreaked upon it their passions. The furniture was chipped and bruised; the couch, distorted by bursting springs, seemed a horrible monster that had been slain during the stress of some grotesque convulsion. Some more potent upheaval had cloven a great slice from the marble mantel. Each plank in the floor owned its particular cant and shriek as from a separate and individual agony. It seemed incredible that all this malice and injury had been wrought upon the room by those who had called it for a time their home; and yet it may have been the cheated home instinct surviving blindly, the resentful rage at false household gods that had kindled their wrath. A hut that is our own we can sweep and adorn and cherish.

The young tenant in the chair allowed these thoughts to file, soft-shod, through his mind, while there drifted into the room furnished sounds and furnished scents. He heard in one room a tittering and incontinent, slack laughter; in others the monologue of a scold, the rattling of dice, a lullaby, and one crying dully; above him a banjo tinkled with spirit. Doors banged somewhere; the elevated trains roared intermittently; a cat yowled miserably upon a back fence. And he breathed the breath of the house—a dank savour rather than a smell—a cold, musty effluvium as from underground vaults mingled with the reeking exhalations of linoleum and mildewed and rotten woodwork.

Then, suddenly, as he rested there, the room was filled with the strong, sweet odour of mignonette. It came as upon a single buffet of wind with such sureness and fragrance and emphasis that it almost seemed a living visitant. And the man cried aloud: "What, dear?" as if he had been called, and sprang up and faced about. The rich odour clung to him and wrapped him around. He reached out his arms for it, all his senses for the time confused and commingled. How could one be peremptorily called by an odour? Surely it must have been a sound. But, was it not the sound that had touched, that had caressed him?

"She has been in this room," he cried, and he sprang to wrest from it a token, for he knew he would recognize the smallest thing that had belonged to her or that she had touched. This enveloping scent of mignonette, the odour that she had loved and made her own—whence came it?

The room had been but carelessly set in order. Scattered upon the flimsy dresser scarf were half a dozen hairpins—those discreet, indistinguishable friends of womankind, feminine of gender, infinite of mood and uncommunicative of tense. These he ignored, conscious of their triumphant lack of identity. Ransacking the drawers of the dresser he came upon a discarded, tiny, ragged handkerchief. He pressed it to his face. It was racy and insolent with heliotrope; he hurled it to the floor. In another drawer he found odd buttons, a theatre programme, a pawnbroker's card, two lost marshmallows, a book on the divination of dreams. In the last was a woman's black satin hair bow, which halted him, poised between ice and fire. But the black satin hair-bow also is femininity's demure, impersonal, common ornament, and tells no tales.

And then he traversed the room like a hound on the scent, skimming the walls, considering the corners of the bulging matting on his hands and knees, rummaging mantel and tables, the curtains and hangings, the drunken cabinet in the corner, for a visible sign, unable to perceive that she was there beside, around, against, within, above him, clinging to him, wooing him, calling him so poignantly through the finer senses that even his grosser ones became cognisant of the call. Once again he answered loudly: "Yes, dear!" and turned, wild-eyed, to gaze on vacancy, for he could not yet discern form and colour and love and outstretched arms in the odour of mignonette. Oh, God! whence that odour, and since when have odours had a voice to call? Thus he groped.

He burrowed in crevices and corners, and found corks and cigarettes. These he passed in passive contempt. But once he found in a fold of the matting a half-smoked cigar, and this he ground beneath his heel with a green and trenchant oath. He sifted the room from end to end. He found dreary and ignoble small records of many a peripatetic tenant; but of her whom he sought, and who may have lodged there, and whose spirit seemed to hover there, he found no trace.

And then he thought of the housekeeper.

He ran from the haunted room downstairs and to a door that showed a crack of light. She came out to his knock. He smothered his excitement as best he could.

"Will you tell me, madam," he besought her, "who occupied the room I have before I came?"

"Yes, sir. I can tell you again. 'Twas Sprowls and Mooney, as I said. Miss B'retta Sprowls it was in the theatres, but Missis Mooney she was. My house is well known for respectability. The marriage certificate hung, framed, on a nail over—"

"What kind of a lady was Miss Sprowls—in looks, I mean?"

"Why, black-haired, sir, short, and stout, with a comical face. They left a week ago Tuesday."

"And before they occupied it?"

"Why, there was a single gentleman connected with the draying business. He left owing me a week. Before him was Missis Crowder and her two children, that stayed four months; and back of them was old Mr. Doyle, whose sons paid for him. He kept the room six months. That goes back a year, sir, and further I do not remember."

He thanked her and crept back to his room. The room was dead. The essence that had vivified it was gone. The perfume of mignonette had departed. In its place was the old, stale odour of mouldy house furniture, of atmosphere in storage.

The ebbing of his hope drained his faith. He sat staring at the yellow, singing gaslight. Soon he walked to the bed and began to tear the sheets into strips. With the blade of his knife he drove them tightly into every crevice around windows and door. When all was snug and taut he turned out the light, turned the gas full on again and laid himself gratefully upon the bed.

It was Mrs. McCool's night to go with the can for beer. So she fetched it and sat with Mrs. Purdy in one of those subterranean retreats where house-keepers foregather and the worm dieth seldom.

"I rented out my third floor, back, this evening," said Mrs. Purdy, across a fine circle of foam. "A young man took it. He went up to bed two hours ago."

"Now, did ye, Mrs. Purdy, ma'am?" said Mrs. McCool, with intense admiration. "You do be a wonder for rentin' rooms of that kind. And did ye tell him, then?" she concluded in a husky whisper, laden with mystery.

"Rooms," said Mrs. Purdy, in her furriest tones, "are furnished for to rent. I did not tell him, Mrs. McCool."

"'Tis right ye are, ma'am; 'tis by renting rooms we kape alive. Ye have the rale sense for business, ma'am. There be many people will rayjict the rentin' of a room if they be tould a suicide has been after dyin' in the bed of it."

"As you say, we has our living to be making," remarked Mrs. Purdy.

"Yis, ma'am; 'tis true. 'Tis just one wake ago this day I helped ye lay out the third floor, back. A pretty slip of a colleen she was to be killin' herself wid the gas—a swate little face she had, Mrs. Purdy, ma'am."

"She'd a-been called handsome, as you say," said Mrs. Purdy, assenting but critical, "but for that mole she had a-growin' by her left eyebrow. Do fill up your glass again, Mrs. McCool."

THE BRIEF DÉBUT OF TILDY

If you do not know Bogle's Chop House and Family Restaurant it is your loss. For if you are one of the fortunate ones who dine expensively you should be interested to know how the other half consumes provisions. And if you belong to the half to whom waiters' checks are things of moment, you should know Bogle's, for there you get your money's worth—in quantity, at least.

Bogle's is situated in that highway of bourgeoisie, that boulevard of Brown-Jones-and-Robinson, Eighth Avenue. There are two rows of tables in the room, six in each row. On each table is a caster-stand, containing cruets of condiments and seasons. From the pepper cruet you may shake a cloud of something tasteless and melancholy, like volcanic dust. From the salt cruet you may expect nothing. Though a man should extract a sanguinary stream from the pallid turnip, yet will his prowess be balked when he comes to wrest salt from Bogle's cruets. Also upon each table stands the counterfeit of that benign sauce made "from the recipe of a nobleman in India."

At the cashier's desk sits Bogle, cold, sordid, slow, smouldering, and takes your money. Behind a mountain of toothpicks he makes your change, files your check, and ejects at you, like a toad, a word about the weather. Beyond a corroboration of his meteorological statement you would better not venture. You are not Bogle's friend; you are a fed, transient customer, and you and he may not meet again until the blowing of Gabriel's dinner horn. So take your change and go—to the devil if you like. There you have Bogle's sentiments.

The needs of Bogle's customers were supplied by two waitresses and a Voice. One of the waitresses was named Aileen. She was tall, beautiful, lively, gracious and learned in persiflage. Her other name? There was no more necessity for another name at Bogle's than there was for finger-bowls.

The name of the other waitress was Tildy. Why do you suggest Matilda? Please listen this time—Tildy—Tildy. Tildy was dumpy, plain-faced, and too anxious to please to please. Repeat the last clause to yourself once or twice, and make the acquaintance of the duplicate infinite.

The Voice at Bogle's was invisible. It came from the kitchen, and did not shine in the way of originality. It was a heathen Voice, and contented itself with vain repetitions of exclamations emitted by the waitresses concerning food.

Will it tire you to be told again that Aileen was beautiful? Had she donned a few hundred dollars' worth of clothes and joined the Easter parade, and had you seen her, you would have hastened to say so yourself.

The customers at Bogle's were her slaves. Six tables full she could wait upon at once. They who were in a hurry restrained their impatience for the joy of merely gazing upon her swiftly moving, graceful figure. They who had finished eating ate more that they might continue in the light of her smiles. Every man there—and they were mostly men—tried to make his impression upon her.

Aileen could successfully exchange repartee against a dozen at once. And every smile that she sent forth lodged, like pellets from a scatter-gun, in as many hearts. And all this while she would be performing astounding feats with orders of pork and beans, pot roasts, ham-and, sausage-and-the-wheats, and any quantity of things on the iron and in the pan and straight up and on the side. With all this feasting and flirting and merry exchange of wit Bogle's came mighty near being a salon, with Aileen for its Madame Récamier.

If the transients were entranced by the fascinating Aileen, the regulars were her adorers. There was much rivalry among many of the steady customers. Aileen could have had an engagement every evening. At least twice a week some one took her to a theatre or to a dance. One stout gentleman whom she and Tildy had privately christened "The Hog" presented her with a turquoise ring. Another one known as "Freshy," who rode on the Traction Company's repair wagon, was going to give her a poodle as soon as his brother got the hauling contract in the Ninth. And the man who always ate spareribs and spinach and said he was a stock broker asked her to go to "Parsifal" with him.

"I don't know where this place is," said Aileen while talking it over with Tildy, "but the wedding-ring's got to be on before I put a stitch into a travelling dress—ain't that right? Well, I guess!"

But, Tildy!

In steaming, chattering, cabbage-scented Bogle's there was almost a heart tragedy. Tildy with the blunt nose, the hay-coloured hair, the freckled skin, the bag-o'-meal figure, had never had an admirer. Not a man followed her with his eyes when she went to and fro in the restaurant save now and then when they glared with the beast-hunger for food. None of them bantered her gaily to coquettish interchanges of wit. None of them loudly "jollied" her of mornings as they did Aileen, accusing her, when the eggs were slow in coming, of late hours in the company of envied swains. No one had ever given her a turquoise ring or invited her upon a voyage to mysterious, distant "Parsifal."

Tildy was a good waitress, and the men tolerated her. They who sat at her tables spoke to her briefly with quotations from the bill of fare; and then raised their voices in honeyed and otherwise-flavoured accents, eloquently addressed to the fair Aileen. They writhed in their chairs to gaze around and over the impending form of Tildy, that Aileen's pulchritude might season and make ambrosia of their bacon and eggs.

And Tildy was content to be the unwooed drudge if Aileen could receive the flattery and the homage. The blunt nose was loyal to the short Grecian. She was Aileen's friend; and she was glad to see her rule hearts and wean the attention of men from smoking pot-pie and lemon meringue. But deep below our freckles and hay-coloured hair the unhandsomest of us dream of a prince or a princess, not vicarious, but coming to us alone.

There was a morning when Aileen tripped in to work with a slightly bruised eye; and Tildy's solicitude was almost enough to heal any optic.

"Fresh guy," explained Aileen, "last night as I was going home at Twenty-third and Sixth. Sashayed up, so he did, and made a break. I turned him down, cold, and he made a sneak; but followed me down to Eighteenth, and tried his hot air again. Gee! but I slapped him a good one, side of the face. Then he give me that eye. Does it look real awful, Til? I should hate that Mr. Nicholson should see it when he comes in for his tea and toast at ten."

Tildy listened to the adventure with breathless admiration. No man had ever tried to follow her. She was safe abroad at any hour of the twenty-four. What bliss it must have been to have had a man follow one and black one's eye for love!

Among the customers at Bogle's was a young man named Seeders, who worked in a laundry office. Mr. Seeders was thin and had light hair, and appeared to have been recently rough-dried and starched. He was too diffident to aspire to Aileen's notice; so he usually sat at one of Tildy's tables, where he devoted himself to silence and boiled weakfish.

One day when Mr. Seeders came in to dinner he had been drinking beer. There were only two or three customers in the restaurant. When Mr. Seeders had finished his weakfish he got up, put his arm around Tildy's waist, kissed her loudly and impudently, walked out upon the street, snapped his fingers in the direction of the laundry, and hied himself to play pennies in the slot machines at the Amusement Arcade.

For a few moments Tildy stood petrified. Then she was aware of Aileen shaking at her an arch forefinger, and saying:

"Why, Til, you naughty girl! Ain't you getting to be awful, Miss Slyboots! First thing I know you'll be stealing some of my fellows. I must keep an eye on you, my lady."

Another thing dawned upon Tildy's recovering wits. In a moment she had advanced from a hopeless, lowly admirer to be an Eve-sister of the potent Aileen. She herself was now a man-charmer, a mark for Cupid, a Sabine who must be coy when the Romans were at their banquet boards. Man had found her waist achievable and her lips desirable. The sudden and amatory Seeders had, as it were, performed for her a miraculous piece of one-day laundry work. He had taken the sackcloth of her uncomeliness, had washed, dried, starched and ironed it, and returned it to her sheer embroidered lawn—the robe of Venus herself.

The freckles on Tildy's cheeks merged into a rosy flush. Now both Circe and Psyche peeped from her brightened eyes. Not even Aileen herself had been publicly embraced and kissed in the restaurant.

Tildy could not keep the delightful secret. When trade was slack she went and stood at Bogle's desk. Her eyes were shining; she tried not to let her words sound proud and boastful.

"A gentleman insulted me to-day," she said. "He hugged me around the waist and kissed me."

"That so?" said Bogle, cracking open his business armour. "After this week you get a dollar a week more."

At the next regular meal when Tildy set food before customers with whom she had acquaintance she said to each of them modestly, as one whose merit needed no bolstering:

"A gentleman insulted me to-day in the restaurant. He put his arm around my waist and kissed me."

The diners accepted the revelation in various ways—some incredulously, some with congratulations; others turned upon her the stream of badinage that had hitherto been directed at Aileen alone. And Tildy's heart swelled in her bosom, for she saw at last the towers of Romance rise above the horizon of the grey plain in which she had for so long travelled.

For two days Mr. Seeders came not again. During that time Tildy established herself firmly as a woman to be wooed. She bought ribbons, and arranged her hair like Aileen's, and tightened her waist two inches. She had a thrilling but delightful fear that Mr. Seeders would rush in suddenly and shoot her with a pistol. He must have loved her desperately; and impulsive lovers are always blindly jealous.

Even Aileen had not been shot at with a pistol. And then Tildy rather hoped that he would not shoot at her, for she was always loyal to Aileen; and she did not want to overshadow her friend.

At 4 o'clock on the afternoon of the third day Mr. Seeders came in. There were no customers at the tables. At the back end of the restaurant Tildy was refilling the mustard pots and Aileen was quartering pies. Mr. Seeders walked back to where they stood.

Tildy looked up and saw him, gasped, and pressed the mustard spoon against her heart. A red hair-bow was in her hair; she wore Venus's Eighth Avenue badge, the blue bead necklace with the swinging silver symbolic heart.

Mr. Seeders was flushed and embarrassed. He plunged one hand into his hip pocket and the other into a fresh pumpkin pie.

"Miss Tildy," said he, "I want to apologise for what I done the other evenin'. Tell you the truth, I was pretty well tanked up or I wouldn't of done it. I wouldn't do no lady that a-way when I was sober. So I hope, Miss Tildy, you'll accept my 'pology, and believe that I wouldn't of done it if I'd known what I was doin' and hadn't of been drunk."

With this handsome plea Mr. Seeders backed away, and departed, feeling that reparation had been made.

But behind the convenient screen Tildy had thrown herself flat upon a table among the butter chips and the coffee cups, and was sobbing her heart out—out and back again to the grey plain wherein travel they with blunt noses and hay-coloured hair. From her knot she had torn the red hair-bow and cast it upon the floor. Seeders she despised utterly; she had but taken his kiss as that of a pioneer and prophetic prince who might have set the clocks going and the pages to running in fairyland. But the kiss had been maudlin and unmeant; the court had not stirred at the false alarm; she must forevermore remain the Sleeping Beauty.

Yet not all was lost. Aileen's arm was around her; and Tildy's red hand groped among the butter chips till it found the warm clasp of her friend's.

"Don't you fret, Til," said Aileen, who did not understand entirely. "That turnip-faced little clothespin of a Seeders ain't worth it. He ain't anything of a gentleman or he wouldn't ever of apologised."

FROM THE CABBY'S SEAT

The cabby has his point of view. It is more single-minded, perhaps, than that of a follower of any other calling. From the high, swaying seat of his hansom he looks upon his fellow-men as nomadic particles, of no account except when possessed of migratory desires. He is Jehu, and you are goods in transit. Be you President or vagabond, to cabby you are only a Fare, he takes you up, cracks his whip, joggles your vertebrae and sets you down.

When time for payment arrives, if you exhibit a familiarity with legal rates you come to know what contempt is; if you find that you have left your pocketbook behind you are made to realise the mildness of Dante's imagination.

It is not an extravagant theory that the cabby's singleness of purpose and concentrated view of life are the results of the hansom's peculiar construction. The cock-of-the-roost sits aloft like Jupiter on an unsharable seat, holding your fate between two thongs of inconstant leather. Helpless, ridiculous, confined, bobbing like a toy mandarin, you sit like a rat in a trap—you, before whom butlers cringe on solid land—and must squeak upward through a slit in your peripatetic sarcophagus to make your feeble wishes known.

Then, in a cab, you are not even an occupant; you are contents. You are a cargo at sea, and the "cherub that sits up aloft" has Davy Jones's street and number by heart.

One night there were sounds of revelry in the big brick tenement-house next door but one to McGary's Family Café. The sounds seemed to emanate from the apartments of the Walsh family. The sidewalk was obstructed by an assortment of interested neighbours, who opened a lane from time to time for a hurrying messenger bearing from McGary's goods pertinent to festivity and diversion. The sidewalk contingent was engaged in comment and discussion from which it made no effort to eliminate the news that Norah Walsh was being married.

In the fulness of time there was an eruption of the merry-makers to the sidewalk. The uninvited guests enveloped and permeated them, and upon the night air rose joyous cries, congratulations, laughter and unclassified noises born of McGary's oblations to the hymeneal scene.

Close to the curb stood Jerry O'Donovan's cab. Night-hawk was Jerry called; but no more lustrous or cleaner hansom than his ever closed its doors upon point lace and November violets. And Jerry's horse! I am within bounds when I tell you that he was stuffed with oats until one of those old ladies who leave their dishes unwashed at home and go about having expressmen arrested, would have smiled—yes, smiled— to have seen him.

Among the shifting, sonorous, pulsing crowd glimpses could be had of Jerry's high hat, battered by the winds and rains of many years; of his nose like a carrot, battered by the frolicsome, athletic progeny of millionaires and by contumacious fares; of his brass-buttoned green coat, admired in the vicinity of McGary's. It was plain that Jerry had usurped the functions of his cab, and was carrying a "load." Indeed, the figure may be extended and he be likened to a bread-waggon if we admit the testimony of a youthful spectator, who was heard to remark "Jerry has got a bun."

From somewhere among the throng in the street or else out of the thin stream of pedestrians a young woman tripped and stood by the cab. The professional hawk's eye of Jerry caught the movement. He made a lurch for the cab, overturning three or four onlookers and himself—no! he caught the cap of a water-plug and kept his feet. Like a sailor shinning up the ratlins during a squall Jerry mounted to his professional seat. Once he was there McGary's liquids were baffled. He seesawed on the mizzenmast of his craft as safe as a Steeple Jack rigged to the flagpole of a skyscraper.

"Step in, lady," said Jerry, gathering his lines. The young woman stepped into the cab; the doors shut with a bang; Jerry's whip cracked in the air; the crowd in the gutter scattered, and the fine hansom dashed away 'crosstown.

When the oat-spry horse had hedged a little his first spurt of speed Jerry broke the lid of his cab and called down through the aperture in the voice of a cracked megaphone, trying to please:

"Where, now, will ye be drivin' to?"

"Anywhere you please," came up the answer, musical and contented.

"'Tis drivin' for pleasure she is," thought Jerry. And then he suggested as a matter of course:

"Take a thrip around in the park, lady. 'Twill be ilegant cool and fine."

"Just as you like," answered the fare, pleasantly.

The cab headed for Fifth avenue and sped up that perfect street. Jerry bounced and swayed in his seat. The potent fluids of McGary were disquieted and they sent new fumes to his head. He sang an ancient song of Killisnook and brandished his whip like a baton.

Inside the cab the fare sat up straight on the cushions, looking to right and left at the lights and houses. Even in the shadowed hansom her eyes shone like stars at twilight.

When they reached Fifty-ninth street Jerry's head was bobbing and his reins were slack. But his horse turned in through the park gate and began the old familiar nocturnal round. And then the fare leaned back, entranced, and breathed deep the clean, wholesome odours of grass and leaf and bloom. And the wise beast in the shafts, knowing his ground, struck into his by-the-hour gait and kept to the right of the road.

Habit also struggled successfully against Jerry's increasing torpor. He raised the hatch of his storm-tossed vessel and made the inquiry that cabbies do make in the park.

"Like shtop at the Cas-sino, lady? Gezzer r'freshm's, 'n lish'n the music. Ev'body shtops."

"I think that would be nice," said the fare.

They reined up with a plunge at the Casino entrance. The cab doors flew open. The fare stepped directly upon the floor. At once she was caught in a web of ravishing music and dazzled by a panorama of lights and colours. Some one slipped a little square card into her hand on which was printed a number—34. She looked around and saw her cab twenty yards away already lining up in its place among the waiting mass of carriages, cabs and motor cars. And then a man who seemed to be all shirt-front danced backward before her; and next she was seated at a little table by a railing over which climbed a jessamine vine.

There seemed to be a wordless invitation to purchase; she consulted a collection of small coins in a thin purse, and received from them license to order a glass of beer. There she sat, inhaling and absorbing it all—the new-coloured, new-shaped life in a fairy palace in an enchanted wood.

At fifty tables sat princes and queens clad in all the silks and gems of the world. And now and then one of them would look curiously at Jerry's fare. They saw a plain figure dressed in a pink silk of the kind that is tempered by the word "foulard," and a plain face that wore a look of love of life that the queens envied.

Twice the long hands of the clocks went round, Royalties thinned from their al fresco thrones, and buzzed or clattered away in their vehicles of state. The music retired into cases of wood and bags of leather and baize. Waiters removed cloths pointedly near the plain figure sitting almost alone.

Jerry's fare rose, and held out her numbered card simply:

"Is there anything coming on the ticket?" she asked.

A waiter told her it was her cab check, and that she should give it to the man at the entrance. This man took it, and called the number. Only three hansoms stood in line. The driver of one of them went and routed out Jerry asleep in his cab. He swore deeply, climbed to the captain's bridge and steered his craft to the pier. His fare entered, and the cab whirled into the cool fastnesses of the park along the shortest homeward cuts.

At the gate a glimmer of reason in the form of sudden suspicion seized upon Jerry's beclouded mind. One or two things occurred to him. He stopped his horse, raised the trap and dropped his phonographic voice, like a lead plummet, through the aperture:

"I want to see four dollars before goin' any further on th' thrip. Have ye got th' dough?"

"Four dollars!" laughed the fare, softly, "dear me, no. I've only got a few pennies and a dime or two."

Jerry shut down the trap and slashed his oat-fed horse. The clatter of hoofs strangled but could not drown the sound of his profanity. He shouted choking and gurgling curses at the starry heavens; he cut viciously with his whip at passing vehicles; he scattered fierce and ever-changing oaths and imprecations along the streets, so that a late truck driver, crawling homeward, heard and was abashed. But he knew his recourse, and made for it at a gallop.

At the house with the green lights beside the steps he pulled up. He flung wide the cab doors and tumbled heavily to the ground.

"Come on, you," he said, roughly.

His fare came forth with the Casino dreamy smile still on her plain face. Jerry took her by the arm and led her into the police station. A gray-moustached sergeant looked keenly across the desk. He and the cabby were no strangers.

"Sargeant," began Jerry in his old raucous, martyred, thunderous tones of complaint. "I've got a fare here that—"

Jerry paused. He drew a knotted, red hand across his brow. The fog set up by McGary was beginning to clear away.

"A fare, sargeant," he continued, with a grin, "that I want to inthroduce to ye. It's me wife that I married at ould man Walsh's this avening. And a divil of a time we had, 'tis thrue. Shake hands wid th' sargeant, Norah, and we'll be off to home."

Before stepping into the cab Norah sighed profoundly.

"I've had such a nice time, Jerry," said she.

AN UNFINISHED STORY

We no longer groan and heap ashes upon our heads when the flames of Tophet are mentioned. For, even the preachers have begun to tell us that God is radium, or ether or some scientific compound, and that the worst we wicked ones may expect is a chemical reaction. This is a pleasing hypothesis; but there lingers yet some of the old, goodly terror of orthodoxy.

There are but two subjects upon which one may discourse with a free imagination, and without the possibility of being controverted. You may talk of your dreams; and you may tell what you heard a parrot say. Both Morpheus and the bird are incompetent witnesses; and your listener dare not attack your recital. The baseless fabric of a vision, then, shall furnish my theme—chosen with apologies and regrets instead of the more limited field of pretty Polly's small talk.

I had a dream that was so far removed from the higher criticism that it had to do with the ancient, respectable, and lamented bar-of-judgment theory.

Gabriel had played his trump; and those of us who could not follow suit were arraigned for examination. I noticed at one side a gathering of professional bondsmen in solemn black and collars that buttoned behind; but it seemed there was some trouble about their real estate titles; and they did not appear to be getting any of us out.

A fly cop—an angel policeman—flew over to me and took me by the left wing. Near at hand was a group of very prosperous-looking spirits arraigned for judgment.

"Do you belong with that bunch?" the policeman asked.

"Who are they?" was my answer.

"Why," said he, "they are—"

But this irrelevant stuff is taking up space that the story should occupy.

Dulcie worked in a department store. She sold Hamburg edging, or stuffed peppers, or automobiles, or other little trinkets such as they keep in department stores. Of what she earned, Dulcie received six dollars per week. The remainder was credited to her and debited to somebody else's account in the ledger kept by G—— Oh, primal energy, you say, Reverend Doctor—Well then, in the Ledger of Primal Energy.

During her first year in the store, Dulcie was paid five dollars per week. It would be instructive to know how she lived on that amount. Don't care? Very well; probably you are interested in larger amounts. Six dollars is a larger amount. I will tell you how she lived on six dollars per week.

One afternoon at six, when Dulcie was sticking her hat-pin within an eighth of an inch of her medulla oblongata, she said to her chum, Sadie—the girl that waits on you with her left side:

"Say, Sade, I made a date for dinner this evening with Piggy."

"You never did!" exclaimed Sadie admiringly. "Well, ain't you the lucky one? Piggy's an awful swell; and he always takes a girl to swell places. He took Blanche up to the Hoffman House one evening, where they have swell music, and you see a lot of swells. You'll have a swell time, Dulce."

Dulcie hurried homeward. Her eyes were shining, and her cheeks showed the delicate pink of life's—real life's—approaching dawn. It was Friday; and she had fifty cents left of her last week's wages.

The streets were filled with the rush-hour floods of people. The electric lights of Broadway were glowing—calling moths from miles, from leagues, from hundreds of leagues out of darkness around to come in and attend the singeing school. Men in accurate clothes, with faces like those carved on cherry stones by the old salts in sailors' homes, turned and stared at Dulcie as she sped, unheeding, past them. Manhattan, the night-blooming cereus, was beginning to unfold its dead-white, heavy-odoured petals.

Dulcie stopped in a store where goods were cheap and bought an imitation lace collar with her fifty cents. That money was to have been spent otherwise—fifteen cents for supper, ten cents for breakfast, ten cents for lunch. Another dime was to be added to her small store of savings; and five cents was to be squandered for licorice drops—the kind that made your cheek look like the toothache, and last as long. The licorice was an extravagance—almost a carouse—but what is life without pleasures?

Dulcie lived in a furnished room. There is this difference between a furnished room and a boarding-house. In a furnished room, other people do not know it when you go hungry.

Dulcie went up to her room—the third floor back in a West Side brownstone-front. She lit the gas. Scientists tell us that the diamond is the hardest substance known. Their mistake. Landladies know of a compound beside which the diamond is as putty. They pack it in the tips of gas-burners; and one may stand on a chair and dig at it in vain until one's fingers are pink and bruised. A hairpin will not remove it; therefore let us call it immovable.

So Dulcie lit the gas. In its one-fourth-candlepower glow we will observe the room.

Couch-bed, dresser, table, washstand, chair—of this much the landlady was guilty. The rest was Dulcie's. On the dresser were her treasures—a gilt china vase presented to her by Sadie, a calendar issued by a pickle works, a book on the divination of dreams, some rice powder in a glass dish, and a cluster of artificial cherries tied with a pink ribbon.

Against the wrinkly mirror stood pictures of General Kitchener, William Muldoon, the Duchess of Marlborough, and Benvenuto Cellini. Against one wall was a plaster of Paris plaque of an O'Callahan in a Roman helmet. Near it was a violent oleograph of a lemon-coloured child assaulting an inflammatory butterfly. This was Dulcie's final judgment in art; but it had never been upset. Her rest had never been disturbed by whispers of stolen copes; no critic had elevated his eyebrows at her infantile entomologist.

Piggy was to call for her at seven. While she swiftly makes ready, let us discreetly face the other way and gossip.

For the room, Dulcie paid two dollars per week. On week-days her breakfast cost ten cents; she made coffee and cooked an egg over the gaslight while she was dressing. On Sunday mornings she feasted royally on veal chops and pineapple fritters at "Billy's" restaurant, at a cost of twenty-five cents—and tipped the waitress ten cents. New York presents so many temptations for one to run into extravagance. She had her lunches in the department-store restaurant at a cost of sixty cents for the week; dinners were $1.05. The evening papers—show me a New Yorker going without his daily paper!—came to six cents; and two Sunday papers—one for the personal column and the other to read—were ten cents. The total amounts to $4.76. Now, one has to buy clothes, and—

I give it up. I hear of wonderful bargains in fabrics, and of miracles performed with needle and thread; but I am in doubt. I hold my pen poised in vain when I would add to Dulcie's life some of those joys that belong to woman by virtue of all the unwritten, sacred, natural, inactive ordinances of the equity of heaven. Twice she had been to Coney Island and had ridden the hobby-horses. 'Tis a weary thing to count your pleasures by summers instead of by hours.

Piggy needs but a word. When the girls named him, an undeserving stigma was cast upon the noble family of swine. The words-of-three-letters lesson in the old blue spelling book begins with Piggy's biography. He was fat; he had the soul of a rat, the habits of a bat, and the magnanimity of a cat . . . He wore expensive clothes; and was a connoisseur in starvation. He could look at a shop-girl and tell you to an hour how long it had been since she had eaten anything more nourishing than marshmallows and tea. He hung about the shopping districts, and prowled around in department stores with his invitations to dinner. Men who escort dogs upon the streets at the end of a string look down upon him. He is a type; I can dwell upon him no longer; my pen is not the kind intended for him; I am no carpenter.

At ten minutes to seven Dulcie was ready. She looked at herself in the wrinkly mirror. The reflection was satisfactory. The dark blue dress, fitting without a wrinkle, the hat with its jaunty black feather, the but-slightly-soiled gloves—all representing self-denial, even of food itself—were vastly becoming.

Dulcie forgot everything else for a moment except that she was beautiful, and that life was about to lift a corner of its mysterious veil for her to observe its wonders. No gentleman had ever asked her out before. Now she was going for a brief moment into the glitter and exalted show.

The girls said that Piggy was a "spender." There would be a grand dinner, and music, and splendidly dressed ladies to look at, and things to eat that strangely twisted the girls' jaws when they tried to tell about them. No doubt she would be asked out again. There was a blue pongee suit in a window that she knew—by saving twenty cents a week instead of ten, in—let's see—Oh, it would run into years! But there was a second-hand store in Seventh Avenue where—

Somebody knocked at the door. Dulcie opened it. The landlady stood there with a spurious smile, sniffing for cooking by stolen gas.

"A gentleman's downstairs to see you," she said. "Name is Mr. Wiggins."

By such epithet was Piggy known to unfortunate ones who had to take him seriously.

Dulcie turned to the dresser to get her handkerchief; and then she stopped still, and bit her underlip hard. While looking in her mirror she had seen fairyland and herself, a princess, just awakening from a long slumber. She had forgotten one that was watching her with sad, beautiful, stern eyes—the only one there was to approve or condemn what she did. Straight and slender and tall, with a look of sorrowful reproach on his handsome, melancholy face, General Kitchener fixed his wonderful eyes on her out of his gilt photograph frame on the dresser.

Dulcie turned like an automatic doll to the landlady.

"Tell him I can't go," she said dully. "Tell him I'm sick, or something. Tell him I'm not going out."

After the door was closed and locked, Dulcie fell upon her bed, crushing her black tip, and cried for ten minutes. General Kitchener was her only friend. He was Dulcie's ideal of a gallant knight. He looked as if he might have a secret sorrow, and his wonderful moustache was a dream, and she was a little afraid of that stern yet tender look in his eyes. She used to have little fancies that he would call at the house sometime, and ask for her, with his sword clanking against his high boots. Once, when a boy was rattling a piece of chain against a lamp-post she had opened the window and looked out. But there was no use. She knew that General Kitchener was away over in Japan, leading his army against the savage Turks; and he would never step out of his gilt frame for her. Yet one look from him had vanquished Piggy that night. Yes, for that night.

When her cry was over Dulcie got up and took off her best dress, and put on her old blue kimono. She wanted no dinner. She sang two verses of "Sammy." Then she became intensely interested in a little red speck on the side of her nose. And after that was attended to, she drew up a chair to the rickety table, and told her fortune with an old deck of cards.

"The horrid, impudent thing!" she said aloud. "And I never gave him a word or a look to make him think it!"

At nine o'clock Dulcie took a tin box of crackers and a little pot of raspberry jam out of her trunk, and had a feast. She offered General Kitchener some jam on a cracker; but he only looked at her as the sphinx would have looked at a butterfly—if there are butterflies in the desert.

"Don't eat it if you don't want to," said Dulcie. "And don't put on so many airs and scold so with your eyes. I wonder if you'd be so superior and snippy if you had to live on six dollars a week."

It was not a good sign for Dulcie to be rude to General Kitchener. And then she turned Benvenuto Cellini face downward with a severe gesture. But that was not inexcusable; for she had always thought he was Henry VIII, and she did not approve of him.

At half-past nine Dulcie took a last look at the pictures on the dresser, turned out the light, and skipped into bed. It's an awful thing to go to bed with a good-night look at General Kitchener, William Muldoon, the Duchess of Marlborough, and Benvenuto Cellini. This story really doesn't get anywhere at all. The rest of it comes later—sometime when Piggy asks Dulcie again to dine with him, and she is feeling lonelier than usual, and General Kitchener happens to be looking the other way; and then—

As I said before, I dreamed that I was standing near a crowd of prosperous-looking angels, and a policeman took me by the wing and asked if I belonged with them.

"Who are they?" I asked.

"Why," said he, "they are the men who hired working-girls, and paid 'em five or six dollars a week to live on. Are you one of the bunch?"

"Not on your immortality," said I. "I'm only the fellow that set fire to an orphan asylum, and murdered a blind man for his pennies."

MAMMON AND THE ARCHER

Old Anthony Rockwall, retired manufacturer and proprietor of Rockwall's Eureka Soap, looked out the library window of his Fifth Avenue mansion and grinned. His neighbour to the right—the aristocratic clubman, G. Van Schuylight Suffolk-Jones—came out to his waiting motor-car, wrinkling a contumelious nostril, as usual, at the Italian renaissance sculpture of the soap palace's front elevation.

"Stuck-up old statuette of nothing doing!" commented the ex-Soap King. "The Eden Musee'll get that old frozen Nesselrode yet if he don't watch out. I'll have this house painted red, white, and blue next summer and see if that'll make his Dutch nose turn up any higher."

And then Anthony Rockwall, who never cared for bells, went to the door of his library and shouted "Mike!" in the same voice that had once chipped off pieces of the welkin on the Kansas prairies.

"Tell my son," said Anthony to the answering menial, "to come in here before he leaves the house."

When young Rockwall entered the library the old man laid aside his newspaper, looked at him with a kindly grimness on his big, smooth, ruddy countenance, rumpled his mop of white hair with one hand and rattled the keys in his pocket with the other.

"Richard," said Anthony Rockwall, "what do you pay for the soap that you use?"

Richard, only six months home from college, was startled a little. He had not yet taken the measure of this sire of his, who was as full of unexpectednesses as a girl at her first party.

"Six dollars a dozen, I think, dad."

"And your clothes?"

"I suppose about sixty dollars, as a rule."

"You're a gentleman," said Anthony, decidedly. "I've heard of these young bloods spending $24 a dozen for soap, and going over the hundred mark for clothes. You've got as much money to waste as any of 'em, and yet you stick to what's decent and moderate. Now I use the old Eureka—not only for sentiment, but it's the purest soap made. Whenever you pay more than 10 cents a cake for soap you buy bad perfumes and labels. But 50 cents is doing very well for a young man in your generation, position and condition. As I said, you're a gentleman. They say it takes three generations to make one. They're off. Money'll do it as slick as soap grease. It's made you one. By hokey! it's almost made one of me. I'm nearly as impolite and disagreeable and ill-mannered as these two old Knickerbocker gents on each side of me that can't sleep of nights because I bought in between 'em."

"There are some things that money can't accomplish," remarked young Rockwall, rather gloomily.

"Now, don't say that," said old Anthony, shocked. "I bet my money on money every time. I've been through the encyclopaedia down to Y looking for something you can't buy with it; and I expect to have to take up the appendix next week. I'm for money against the field. Tell me something money won't buy."

"For one thing," answered Richard, rankling a little, "it won't buy one into the exclusive circles of society."

"Oho! won't it?" thundered the champion of the root of evil. "You tell me where your exclusive circles would be if the first Astor hadn't had the money to pay for his steerage passage over?"

Richard sighed.

"And that's what I was coming to," said the old man, less boisterously. "That's why I asked you to come in. There's something going wrong with you, boy. I've been noticing it for two weeks. Out with it. I guess I could lay my hands on eleven millions within twenty-four hours, besides the real estate. If it's your liver, there's the Rambler down in the bay, coaled, and ready to steam down to the Bahamas in two days."

"Not a bad guess, dad; you haven't missed it far."

"Ah," said Anthony, keenly; "what's her name?"

Richard began to walk up and down the library floor. There was enough comradeship and sympathy in this crude old father of his to draw his confidence.

"Why don't you ask her?" demanded old Anthony. "She'll jump at you. You've got the money and the looks, and you're a decent boy. Your hands are clean. You've got no Eureka soap on 'em. You've been to college, but she'll overlook that."

"I haven't had a chance," said Richard.

"Make one," said Anthony. "Take her for a walk in the park, or a straw ride, or walk home with her from church. Chance! Pshaw!"

"You don't know the social mill, dad. She's part of the stream that turns it. Every hour and minute of her time is arranged for days in advance. I must have that girl, dad, or this town is a blackjack swamp forevermore. And I can't write it—I can't do that."

"Tut!" said the old man. "Do you mean to tell me that with all the money I've got you can't get an hour or two of a girl's time for yourself?"

"I've put it off too late. She's going to sail for Europe at noon day after to-morrow for a two years' stay. I'm to see her alone to-morrow evening for a few minutes. She's at Larchmont now at her aunt's. I can't go there. But I'm allowed to meet her with a cab at the Grand Central Station to-morrow evening at the 8.30 train. We drive down Broadway to Wallack's at a gallop, where her mother and a box party will be waiting for us in the lobby. Do you think she would listen to a declaration from me during that six or eight minutes under those circumstances? No. And what chance would I have in the theatre or afterward? None. No, dad, this is one tangle that your money can't unravel. We can't buy one minute of time with cash; if we could, rich people would live longer. There's no hope of getting a talk with Miss Lantry before she sails."

"All right, Richard, my boy," said old Anthony, cheerfully. "You may run along down to your club now. I'm glad it ain't your liver. But don't forget to burn a few punk sticks in the joss house to the great god Mazuma from time to time. You say money won't buy time? Well, of course, you can't order eternity wrapped up and delivered at your residence for a price, but I've seen Father Time get pretty bad stone bruises on his heels when he walked through the gold diggings."

That night came Aunt Ellen, gentle, sentimental, wrinkled, sighing, oppressed by wealth, in to Brother Anthony at his evening paper, and began discourse on the subject of lovers' woes.

"He told me all about it," said brother Anthony, yawning. "I told him my bank account was at his service. And then he began to knock money. Said money couldn't help. Said the rules of society couldn't be bucked for a yard by a team of ten-millionaires."

"Oh, Anthony," sighed Aunt Ellen, "I wish you would not think so much of money. Wealth is nothing where a true affection is concerned. Love is all-powerful. If he only had spoken earlier! She could not have refused our Richard. But now I fear it is too late. He will have no opportunity to address her. All your gold cannot bring happiness to your son."

At eight o'clock the next evening Aunt Ellen took a quaint old gold ring from a moth-eaten case and gave it to Richard.

"Wear it to-night, nephew," she begged. "Your mother gave it to me. Good luck in love she said it brought. She asked me to give it to you when you had found the one you loved."

Young Rockwall took the ring reverently and tried it on his smallest finger. It slipped as far as the second joint and stopped. He took it off and stuffed it into his vest pocket, after the manner of man. And then he 'phoned for his cab.

At the station he captured Miss Lantry out of the gadding mob at eight thirty-two.

"We mustn't keep mamma and the others waiting," said she.

"To Wallack's Theatre as fast as you can drive!" said Richard loyally.

They whirled up Forty-second to Broadway, and then down the white-starred lane that leads from the soft meadows of sunset to the rocky hills of morning.

At Thirty-fourth Street young Richard quickly thrust up the trap and ordered the cabman to stop.

"I've dropped a ring," he apologised, as he climbed out. "It was my mother's, and I'd hate to lose it. I won't detain you a minute—I saw where it fell."

In less than a minute he was back in the cab with the ring.

But within that minute a crosstown car had stopped directly in front of the cab. The cabman tried to pass to the left, but a heavy express wagon cut him off. He tried the right, and had to back away from a furniture van that had no business to be there. He tried to back out, but dropped his reins and swore dutifully. He was blockaded in a tangled mess of vehicles and horses.

One of those street blockades had occurred that sometimes tie up commerce and movement quite suddenly in the big city.

"Why don't you drive on?" said Miss Lantry, impatiently. "We'll be late."

Richard stood up in the cab and looked around. He saw a congested flood of wagons, trucks, cabs, vans and street cars filling the vast space where Broadway, Sixth Avenue and Thirty-fourth street cross one another as a twenty-six inch maiden fills her twenty-two inch girdle. And still from all the cross streets they were hurrying and rattling toward the converging point at full speed, and hurling themselves into the struggling mass, locking wheels and adding their drivers' imprecations to the clamour. The entire traffic of Manhattan seemed to have jammed itself around them. The oldest New Yorker among the thousands of spectators that lined the sidewalks had not witnessed a street blockade of the proportions of this one.

"I'm very sorry," said Richard, as he resumed his seat, "but it looks as if we are stuck. They won't get this jumble loosened up in an hour. It was my fault. If I hadn't dropped the ring we—"

"Let me see the ring," said Miss Lantry. "Now that it can't be helped, I don't care. I think theatres are stupid, anyway."

At 11 o'clock that night somebody tapped lightly on Anthony Rockwall's door.

"Come in," shouted Anthony, who was in a red dressing-gown, reading a book of piratical adventures.

Somebody was Aunt Ellen, looking like a grey-haired angel that had been left on earth by mistake.

"They're engaged, Anthony," she said, softly. "She has promised to marry our Richard. On their way to the theatre there was a street blockade, and it was two hours before their cab could get out of it.

"And oh, brother Anthony, don't ever boast of the power of money again. A little emblem of true love—a little ring that symbolised unending and unmercenary affection—was the cause of our Richard finding his happiness. He dropped it in the street, and got out to recover it. And before they could continue the blockade occurred. He spoke to his love and won her there while the cab was hemmed in. Money is dross compared with true love, Anthony."

"All right," said old Anthony. "I'm glad the boy has got what he wanted. I told him I wouldn't spare any expense in the matter if—"

"But, brother Anthony, what good could your money have done?"

"Sister," said Anthony Rockwall. "I've got my pirate in a devil of a scrape. His ship has just been scuttled, and he's too good a judge of the value of money to let drown. I wish you would let me go on with this chapter."

The story should end here. I wish it would as heartily as you who read it wish it did. But we must go to the bottom of the well for truth.

The next day a person with red hands and a blue polka-dot necktie, who called himself Kelly, called at Anthony Rockwall's house, and was at once received in the library.

"Well," said Anthony, reaching for his chequebook, "it was a good bilin' of soap. Let's see—you had $5,000 in cash."

"I paid out $300 more of my own," said Kelly. "I had to go a little above the estimate. I got the express wagons and cabs mostly for $5; but the trucks and two-horse teams mostly raised me to $10. The motormen wanted $10, and some of the loaded teams $20. The cops struck me hardest—$50 I paid two, and the rest $20 and $25. But didn't it work beautiful, Mr. Rockwall? I'm glad William A. Brady wasn't onto that little outdoor vehicle mob scene. I wouldn't want William to break his heart with jealousy. And never a rehearsal, either! The boys was on time to the fraction of a second. It was two hours before a snake could get below Greeley's statue."

"Thirteen hundred—there you are, Kelly," said Anthony, tearing off a check. "Your thousand, and the $300 you were out. You don't despise money, do you, Kelly?"

"Me?" said Kelly. "I can lick the man that invented poverty."

Anthony called Kelly when he was at the door.

"You didn't notice," said he, "anywhere in the tie-up, a kind of a fat boy without any clothes on shooting arrows around with a bow, did you?"

"Why, no," said Kelly, mystified. "I didn't. If he was like you say, maybe the cops pinched him before I got there."

"I thought the little rascal wouldn't be on hand," chuckled Anthony. "Good-by, Kelly."

LOST ON DRESS PARADE

Mr. Towers Chandler was pressing his evening suit in his hall bedroom. One iron was heating on a small gas stove; the other was being pushed vigorously back and forth to make the desirable crease that would be seen later on extending in straight lines from Mr. Chandler's patent leather shoes to the edge of his low-cut vest. So much of the hero's toilet may be intrusted to our confidence. The remainder may be guessed by those whom genteel poverty has driven to ignoble expedient. Our next view of him shall be as he descends the steps of his lodging-house immaculately and correctly clothed; calm, assured, handsome—in appearance the typical New York young clubman setting out, slightly bored, to inaugurate the pleasures of the evening.

Chandler's honorarium was $18 per week. He was employed in the office of an architect. He was twenty-two years old; he considered architecture to be truly an art; and he honestly believed—though he would not have dared to admit it in New York—that the Flatiron Building was inferior in design to the great cathedral in Milan.

Out of each week's earnings Chandler set aside $1. At the end of each ten weeks with the extra capital thus accumulated, he purchased one gentleman's evening from the bargain counter of stingy old Father Time. He arrayed himself in the regalia of millionaires and presidents;

he took himself to the quarter where life is brightest and showiest, and there dined with taste and luxury. With ten dollars a man may, for a few hours, play the wealthy idler to perfection. The sum is ample for a well-considered meal, a bottle bearing a respectable label, commensurate tips, a smoke, cab fare and the ordinary etceteras.

This one delectable evening culled from each dull seventy was to Chandler a source of renascent bliss. To the society bud comes but one début; it stands alone sweet in her memory when her hair has whitened; but to Chandler each ten weeks brought a joy as keen, as thrilling, as new as the first had been. To sit among bon vivants under palms in the swirl of concealed music, to look upon the habitués of such a paradise and to be looked upon by them—what is a girl's first dance and short-sleeved tulle compared with this?

Up Broadway Chandler moved with the vespertine dress parade. For this evening he was an exhibit as well as a gazer. For the next sixty-nine evenings he would be dining in cheviot and worsted at dubious table d'hôtes, at whirlwind lunch counters, on sandwiches and beer in his hall-bedroom. He was willing to do that, for he was a true son of the great city of razzle-dazzle, and to him one evening in the limelight made up for many dark ones.

Chandler protracted his walk until the Forties began to intersect the great and glittering primrose way, for the evening was yet young, and when one is of the beau monde only one day in seventy, one loves to protract the pleasure. Eyes bright, sinister, curious, admiring, provocative, alluring were bent upon him, for his garb and air proclaimed him a devotee to the hour of solace and pleasure.

At a certain corner he came to a standstill, proposing to himself the question of turning back toward the showy and fashionable restaurant in which he usually dined on the evenings of his especial luxury. Just then a girl scuddled lightly around the corner, slipped on a patch of icy snow and fell plump upon the sidewalk.

Chandler assisted her to her feet with instant and solicitous courtesy. The girl hobbled to the wall of the building, leaned against it, and thanked him demurely.

"I think my ankle is strained," she said. "It twisted when I fell."

"Does it pain you much?" inquired Chandler.

"Only when I rest my weight upon it. I think I will be able to walk in a minute or two."

"If I can be of any further service," suggested the young man, "I will call a cab, or—"

"Thank you," said the girl, softly but heartily. "I am sure you need not trouble yourself any further. It was so awkward of me. And my shoe heels are horridly common-sense; I can't blame them at all."

Chandler looked at the girl and found her swiftly drawing his interest. She was pretty in a refined way; and her eye was both merry and kind. She was inexpensively clothed in a plain black dress that suggested a sort of uniform such as shop girls wear. Her glossy dark-brown hair showed its coils beneath a cheap hat of black straw whose only ornament was a velvet ribbon and bow. She could have posed as a model for the self-respecting working girl of the best type.

A sudden idea came into the head of the young architect. He would ask this girl to dine with him. Here was the element that his splendid but solitary periodic feasts had lacked. His brief season of elegant luxury would be doubly enjoyable if he could add to it a lady's society. This girl was a lady, he was sure—her manner and speech settled that. And in spite of her extremely plain attire he felt that he would be pleased to sit at table with her.

These thoughts passed swiftly through his mind, and he decided to ask her. It was a breach of etiquette, of course, but oftentimes wage-earning girls waived formalities in matters of this kind. They were generally shrewd judges of men; and thought better of their own judgment than they did of useless conventions. His ten dollars, discreetly expended, would enable the two to dine very well indeed. The dinner would no doubt be a wonderful experience thrown into the dull routine of the girl's life; and her lively appreciation of it would add to his own triumph and pleasure.

"I think," he said to her, with frank gravity, "that your foot needs a longer rest than you suppose. Now, I am going to suggest a way in which you can give it that and at the same time do me a favour. I was on my way to dine all by my lonely self when you came tumbling around the corner. You come with me and we'll have a cozy dinner and a pleasant talk together, and by that time your game ankle will carry you home very nicely, I am sure."

The girl looked quickly up into Chandler's clear, pleasant countenance. Her eyes twinkled once very brightly, and then she smiled ingenuously.

"But we don't know each other—it wouldn't be right, would it?" she said, doubtfully.

"There is nothing wrong about it," said the young man, candidly. "I'll introduce myself—permit me—Mr. Towers Chandler. After our dinner, which I will try to make as pleasant as possible, I will bid you good-evening, or attend you safely to your door, whichever you prefer."

"But, dear me!" said the girl, with a glance at Chandler's faultless attire. "In this old dress and hat!"

"Never mind that," said Chandler, cheerfully. "I'm sure you look more charming in them than any one we shall see in the most elaborate dinner toilette."

"My ankle does hurt yet," admitted the girl, attempting a limping step. "I think I will accept your invitation, Mr. Chandler. You may call me—Miss Marian."

"Come then, Miss Marian," said the young architect, gaily, but with perfect courtesy; "you will not have far to walk. There is a very respectable and good restaurant in the next block. You will have to lean on my arm—so—and walk slowly. It is lonely dining all by one's self. I'm just a little bit glad that you slipped on the ice."

When the two were established at a well-appointed table, with a promising waiter hovering in attendance, Chandler began to experience the real joy that his regular outing always brought to him.

The restaurant was not so showy or pretentious as the one further down Broadway, which he always preferred, but it was nearly so. The tables were well filled with prosperous-looking diners, there was a good orchestra, playing softly enough to make conversation a possible pleasure, and the cuisine and service were beyond criticism. His companion, even in her cheap hat and dress, held herself with an air that added distinction to the natural beauty of her face and figure. And it is certain that she looked at Chandler, with his animated but self-possessed manner and his kindling and frank blue eyes, with something not far from admiration in her own charming face.

Then it was that the Madness of Manhattan, the frenzy of Fuss and Feathers, the Bacillus of Brag, the Provincial Plague of Pose seized upon Towers Chandler. He was on Broadway, surrounded by pomp and style, and there were eyes to look at him. On the stage of that comedy he had assumed to play the one-night part of a butterfly of fashion and an idler of means and taste. He was dressed for the part, and all his good angels had not the power to prevent him from acting it.

So he began to prate to Miss Marian of clubs, of teas, of golf and riding and kennels and cotillions and tours abroad and threw out hints of a yacht lying at Larchmont. He could see that she was vastly impressed by this vague talk, so he endorsed his pose by random insinuations concerning great wealth, and mentioned familiarly a few names that are handled reverently by the proletariat. It was Chandler's short little day, and he was wringing from it the best that could be had, as he saw it. And yet once or twice he saw the pure gold of this girl shine through the mist that his egotism had raised between him and all objects.

"This way of living that you speak of," she said, "sounds so futile and purposeless. Haven't you any work to do in the world that might interest you more?"

"My dear Miss Marian," he exclaimed—"work! Think of dressing every day for dinner, of making half a dozen calls in an afternoon—with a policeman at every corner ready to jump into your auto and take you to the station, if you get up any greater speed than a donkey cart's gait. We do-nothings are the hardest workers in the land."

The dinner was concluded, the waiter generously fed, and the two walked out to the corner where they had met. Miss Marian walked very well now; her limp was scarcely noticeable.

"Thank you for a nice time," she said, frankly. "I must run home now. I liked the dinner very much, Mr. Chandler."

He shook hands with her, smiling cordially, and said something about a game of bridge at his club. He watched her for a moment, walking rather rapidly eastward, and then he found a cab to drive him slowly homeward.

In his chilly bedroom Chandler laid away his evening clothes for a sixty-nine days' rest. He went about it thoughtfully.

"That was a stunning girl," he said to himself. "She's all right, too, I'd be sworn, even if she does have to work. Perhaps if I'd told her the truth instead of all that razzle-dazzle we might—but, confound it! I had to play up to my clothes."

Thus spoke the brave who was born and reared in the wigwams of the tribe of the Manhattans.

The girl, after leaving her entertainer, sped swiftly cross-town until she arrived at a handsome and sedate mansion two squares to the east, facing on that avenue which is the highway of Mammon and the auxiliary gods. Here she entered hurriedly and ascended to a room where a handsome young lady in an elaborate house dress was looking anxiously out the window.

"Oh, you madcap!" exclaimed the elder girl, when the other entered. "When will you quit frightening us this way? It is two hours since you ran out in that rag of an old dress and Marie's hat. Mamma has been so alarmed. She sent Louis in the auto to try to find you. You are a bad, thoughtless Puss."

The elder girl touched a button, and a maid came in a moment.

"Marie, tell mamma that Miss Marian has returned."

"Don't scold, sister. I only ran down to Mme. Theo's to tell her to use mauve insertion instead of pink. My costume and Marie's hat were just what I needed. Every one thought I was a shopgirl, I am sure."

"Dinner is over, dear; you stayed so late."

"I know. I slipped on the sidewalk and turned my ankle. I could not walk, so I hobbled into a restaurant and sat there until I was better. That is why I was so long."

The two girls sat in the window seat, looking out at the lights and the stream of hurrying vehicles in the avenue. The younger one cuddled down with her head in her sister's lap.

"We will have to marry some day," she said dreamily—"both of us. We have so much money that we will not be allowed to disappoint the public. Do you want me to tell you the kind of a man I could love, Sis?"

"Go on, you scatterbrain," smiled the other.

"I could love a man with dark and kind blue eyes, who is gentle and respectful to poor girls, who is handsome and good and does not try to flirt. But I could love him only if he had an ambition, an object, some work to do in the world. I would not care how poor he was if I could help him build his way up. But, sister dear, the kind of man we always meet—the man who lives an idle life between society and his clubs—I could not love a man like that, even if his eyes were blue and he were ever so kind to poor girls whom he met in the street."

THE SKYLIGHT ROOM

First Mrs. Parker would show you the double parlours. You would not dare to interrupt her description of their advantages and of the merits of the gentleman who had occupied them for eight years. Then you would manage to stammer forth the confession that you were neither a doctor nor a dentist. Mrs. Parker's manner of receiving the admission was such that you could never afterward entertain the same feeling toward your parents, who had neglected to train you up in one of the professions that fitted Mrs. Parker's parlours.

Next you ascended one flight of stairs and looked at the second-floor-back at $8. Convinced by her second-floor manner that it was worth the $12 that Mr. Toosenberry always paid for it until he left to take charge of his brother's orange plantation in Florida near Palm Beach, where Mrs. McIntyre always spent the winters that had the double front room with private bath, you managed to babble that you wanted something still cheaper.

If you survived Mrs. Parker's scorn, you were taken to look at Mr. Skidder's large hall room on the third floor. Mr. Skidder's room was not vacant. He wrote plays and smoked cigarettes in it all day long. But every room-hunter was made to visit his room to admire the lambrequins. After each visit, Mr. Skidder, from the fright caused by possible eviction, would pay something on his rent.

Then—oh, then—if you still stood on one foot, with your hot hand clutching the three moist dollars in your pocket, and hoarsely proclaimed your hideous and culpable poverty, nevermore would Mrs. Parker be cicerone of yours. She would honk loudly the word "Clara," she would show you her back, and march downstairs. Then Clara, the coloured maid, would escort you up the carpeted ladder that served for the fourth flight, and show you the Skylight Room. It occupied 7×8 feet of floor space at the middle of the hall. On each side of it was a dark lumber closet or storeroom.

In it was an iron cot, a washstand and a chair. A shelf was the dresser. Its four bare walls seemed to close in upon you like the sides of a coffin. Your hand crept to your throat, you gasped, you looked up as from a well—and breathed once more. Through the glass of the little skylight you saw a square of blue infinity.

"Two dollars, suh," Clara would say in her half-contemptuous, half-Tuskegeenial tones.

One day Miss Leeson came hunting for a room. She carried a typewriter made to be lugged around by a much larger lady. She was a very little girl, with eyes and hair that had kept on growing after she had stopped and that always looked as if they were saying: "Goodness me! Why didn't you keep up with us?"

Mrs. Parker showed her the double parlours. "In this closet," she said, "one could keep a skeleton or anaesthetic or coal—"

"But I am neither a doctor nor a dentist," said Miss Leeson, with a shiver.

Mrs. Parker gave her the incredulous, pitying, sneering, icy stare that she kept for those who failed to qualify as doctors or dentists, and led the way to the second floor back.

"Eight dollars?" said Miss Leeson. "Dear me! I'm not Hetty if I do look green. I'm just a poor little working girl. Show me something higher and lower."

Mr. Skidder jumped and strewed the floor with cigarette stubs at the rap on his door.

"Excuse me, Mr. Skidder," said Mrs. Parker, with her demon's smile at his pale looks. "I didn't know you were in. I asked the lady to have a look at your lambrequins."

"They're too lovely for anything," said Miss Leeson, smiling in exactly the way the angels do.

After they had gone Mr. Skidder got very busy erasing the tall, black-haired heroine from his latest (unproduced) play and inserting a small, roguish one with heavy, bright hair and vivacious features.

"Anna Held'll jump at it," said Mr. Skidder to himself, putting his feet up against the lambrequins and disappearing in a cloud of smoke like an aerial cuttlefish.

Presently the tocsin call of "Clara!" sounded to the world the state of Miss Leeson's purse. A dark goblin seized her, mounted a Stygian stairway, thrust her into a vault with a glimmer of light in its top and muttered the menacing and cabalistic words "Two dollars!"

"I'll take it!" sighed Miss Leeson, sinking down upon the squeaky iron bed.

Every day Miss Leeson went out to work. At night she brought home papers with handwriting on them and made copies with her typewriter. Sometimes she had no work at night, and then she would sit on the steps of the high stoop with the other roomers. Miss Leeson was not intended for a sky-light room when the plans were drawn for her creation. She was gay-hearted and full of tender, whimsical fancies. Once she let Mr. Skidder read to her three acts of his great (unpublished) comedy, "It's No Kid; or, The Heir of the Subway."

There was rejoicing among the gentlemen roomers whenever Miss Leeson had time to sit on the steps for an hour or two. But Miss Longnecker, the tall blonde who taught in a public school and said, "Well, really!" to everything you said, sat on the top step and sniffed. And Miss Dorn, who shot at the moving ducks at Coney every Sunday and worked in a department store, sat on the bottom step and sniffed. Miss Leeson sat on the middle step and the men would quickly group around her.

Especially Mr. Skidder, who had cast her in his mind for the star part in a private, romantic (unspoken) drama in real life. And especially Mr. Hoover, who was forty-five, fat, flush and foolish. And especially very young Mr. Evans, who set up a hollow cough to induce her to ask him to leave off cigarettes. The men voted her "the funniest and jolliest ever," but the sniffs on the top step and the lower step were implacable.

I pray you let the drama halt while Chorus stalks to the footlights and drops an epicedian tear upon the fatness of Mr. Hoover. Tune the pipes to the tragedy of tallow, the bane of bulk, the calamity of corpulence. Tried out, Falstaff might have rendered more romance to the ton than would have Romeo's rickety ribs to the ounce. A lover may sigh, but he must not puff. To the train of Momus are the fat men remanded. In vain beats the faithfullest heart above a 52-inch belt. Avaunt, Hoover! Hoover, forty-five, flush and foolish, might carry off Helen herself; Hoover, forty-five, flush, foolish and fat is meat for perdition. There was never a chance for you, Hoover.

As Mrs. Parker's roomers sat thus one summer's evening, Miss Leeson looked up into the firmament and cried with her little gay laugh:

"Why, there's Billy Jackson! I can see him from down here, too."

All looked up—some at the windows of skyscrapers, some casting about for an airship, Jackson-guided.

"It's that star," explained Miss Leeson, pointing with a tiny finger. "Not the big one that twinkles—the steady blue one near it. I can see it every night through my skylight. I named it Billy Jackson."

"Well, really!" said Miss Longnecker. "I didn't know you were an astronomer, Miss Leeson."

"Oh, yes," said the small star gazer, "I know as much as any of them about the style of sleeves they're going to wear next fall in Mars."

"Well, really!" said Miss Longnecker. "The star you refer to is Gamma, of the constellation Cassiopeia. It is nearly of the second magnitude, and its meridian passage is—"

"Oh," said the very young Mr. Evans, "I think Billy Jackson is a much better name for it."

"Same here," said Mr. Hoover, loudly breathing defiance to Miss Longnecker. "I think Miss Leeson has just as much right to name stars as any of those old astrologers had."

"Well, really!" said Miss Longnecker.

"I wonder whether it's a shooting star," remarked Miss Dorn. "I hit nine ducks and a rabbit out of ten in the gallery at Coney Sunday."

"He doesn't show up very well from down here," said Miss Leeson. "You ought to see him from my room. You know you can see stars even in the daytime from the bottom of a well. At night my room is like the shaft of a coal mine, and it makes Billy Jackson look like the big diamond pin that Night fastens her kimono with."

There came a time after that when Miss Leeson brought no formidable papers home to copy. And when she went out in the morning, instead of working, she went from office to office and let her heart melt away in the drip of cold refusals transmitted through insolent office boys. This went on.

There came an evening when she wearily climbed Mrs. Parker's stoop at the hour when she always returned from her dinner at the restaurant. But she had had no dinner.

As she stepped into the hall Mr. Hoover met her and seized his chance. He asked her to marry him, and his fatness hovered above her like an avalanche. She dodged, and caught the balustrade. He tried for her hand, and she raised it and smote him weakly in the face. Step by step she went up, dragging herself by the railing. She passed Mr. Skidder's door as he was red-inking a stage direction for Myrtle Delorme (Miss Leeson) in his (unaccepted) comedy, to "pirouette across stage from L to the side of the Count." Up the carpeted ladder she crawled at last and opened the door of the skylight room.

She was too weak to light the lamp or to undress. She fell upon the iron cot, her fragile body scarcely hollowing the worn springs. And in that Erebus of the skylight room, she slowly raised her heavy eyelids, and smiled.

For Billy Jackson was shining down on her, calm and bright and constant through the skylight. There was no world about her. She was sunk in a pit of blackness, with but that small square of pallid light framing the star that she had so whimsically and oh, so ineffectually named. Miss Longnecker must be right; it was Gamma, of the constellation Cassiopeia, and not Billy Jackson. And yet she could not let it be Gamma.

As she lay on her back she tried twice to raise her arm. The third time she got two thin fingers to her lips and blew a kiss out of the black pit to Billy Jackson. Her arm fell back limply.

"Good-bye, Billy," she murmured faintly. "You're millions of miles away and you won't even twinkle once. But you kept where I could see you most of the time up there when there wasn't anything else but darkness to look at, didn't you? . . . Millions of miles . . . Good-bye, Billy Jackson."

Clara, the coloured maid, found the door locked at 10 the next day, and they forced it open. Vinegar, and the slapping of wrists and burnt feathers proving of no avail, some one ran to 'phone for an ambulance.

In due time it backed up to the door with much gong-clanging, and the capable young medico, in his white linen coat, ready, active, confident, with his smooth face half debonair, half grim, danced up the steps.

"Ambulance call to 49," he said briefly. "What's the trouble?"

"Oh, yes, doctor," sniffed Mrs. Parker, as though her trouble that there should be trouble in the house was the greater. "I can't think what can be the matter with her. Nothing we could do would bring her to. It's a young woman, a Miss Elsie—yes, a Miss Elsie Leeson. Never before in my house—"

"What room?" cried the doctor in a terrible voice, to which Mrs. Parker was a stranger.

"The skylight room. It—"

Evidently the ambulance doctor was familiar with the location of skylight rooms. He was gone up the stairs, four at a time. Mrs. Parker followed slowly, as her dignity demanded.

On the first landing she met him coming back bearing the astronomer in his arms. He stopped and let loose the practised scalpel of his tongue, not loudly. Gradually Mrs. Parker crumpled as a stiff garment that slips down from a nail. Ever afterward there remained crumples in her mind and body. Sometimes her curious roomers would ask her what the doctor said to her.

"Let that be," she would answer. "If I can get forgiveness for having heard it I will be satisfied."

The ambulance physician strode with his burden through the pack of hounds that follow the curiosity chase, and even they fell back along the sidewalk abashed, for his face was that of one who bears his own dead.

They noticed that he did not lay down upon the bed prepared for it in the ambulance the form that he carried, and all that he said was: "Drive like h——l, Wilson," to the driver.

That is all. Is it a story? In the next morning's paper I saw a little news item, and the last sentence of it may help you (as it helped me) to weld the incidents together.

It recounted the reception into Bellevue Hospital of a young woman who had been removed from No. 49 East —— street, suffering from debility induced by starvation. It concluded with these words:

"Dr. William Jackson, the ambulance physician who attended the case, says the patient will recover."

MEMOIRS OF A YELLOW DOG

I don't suppose it will knock any of you people off your perch to read a contribution from an animal. Mr. Kipling and a good many others have demonstrated the fact that animals can express themselves in remunerative English, and no magazine goes to press nowadays without an animal story in it, except the old-style monthlies that are still running pictures of Bryan and the Mont Pélee horror.

But you needn't look for any stuck-up literature in my piece, such as Bearoo, the bear, and Snakoo, the snake, and Tammanoo, the tiger, talk in the jungle books. A yellow dog that's spent most of his life in a cheap New York flat, sleeping in a corner on an old sateen underskirt (the one she spilled port wine on at the Lady Longshoremen's banquet), mustn't be expected to perform any tricks with the art of speech.

I was born a yellow pup; date, locality, pedigree and weight unknown. The first thing I can recollect, an old woman had me in a basket at Broadway and Twenty-third trying to sell me to a fat lady. Old Mother Hubbard was boosting me to beat the band as a genuine Pomeranian-Hambletonian-Red-Irish-Cochin-China-Stoke-Pogis fox terrier. The fat lady chased a V around among the samples of gros grain flannelette in her shopping bag till she cornered it, and gave up. From that moment I was a pet—a mamma's own wootsey squidlums. Say, gentle reader, did you ever have a 200-pound woman breathing a flavour of Camembert cheese and Peau d'Espagne pick you up and wallop her nose all over you, remarking all the time in an Emma Eames tone of voice: "Oh, oo's um oodlum, doodlum, woodlum, toodlum, bitsy-witsy skoodlums?"

From a pedigreed yellow pup I grew up to be an anonymous yellow cur looking like a cross between an Angora cat and a box of lemons. But my mistress never tumbled. She thought that the two primeval pups that Noah chased into the ark were but a collateral branch of my ancestors. It took two policemen to keep her from entering me at the Madison Square Garden for the Siberian bloodhound prize.

I'll tell you about that flat. The house was the ordinary thing in New York, paved with Parian marble in the entrance hall and cobblestones above the first floor. Our flat was three—well, not flights—climbs up. My mistress rented it unfurnished, and put in the regular things— 1903 antique unholstered parlour set, oil chromo of geishas in a Harlem tea house, rubber plant and husband.

By Sirius! there was a biped I felt sorry for. He was a little man with sandy hair and whiskers a good deal like mine. Henpecked?—well, toucans and flamingoes and pelicans all had their bills in him. He wiped the dishes and listened to my mistress tell about the cheap, ragged things the lady with the squirrel-skin coat on the second floor hung out on her line to dry. And every evening while she was getting supper she made him take me out on the end of a string for a walk.

If men knew how women pass the time when they are alone they'd never marry. Laura Lean Jibbey, peanut brittle, a little almond cream on the neck muscles, dishes unwashed, half an hour's talk with the iceman, reading a package of old letters, a couple of pickles and two bottles of malt extract, one hour peeking through a hole in the window shade into the flat across the air-shaft—that's about all there is to it. Twenty minutes before time for him to come home from work she straightens up the house, fixes her rat so it won't show, and gets out a lot of sewing for a ten-minute bluff.

I led a dog's life in that flat. 'Most all day I lay there in my corner watching that fat woman kill time. I slept sometimes and had pipe dreams about being out chasing cats into basements and growling at old ladies with black mittens, as a dog was intended to do. Then she would pounce upon me with a lot of that drivelling poodle palaver and kiss me on the nose—but what could I do? A dog can't chew cloves.

I began to feel sorry for Hubby, dog my cats if I didn't. We looked so much alike that people noticed it when we went out; so we shook the streets that Morgan's cab drives down, and took to climbing the piles of last December's snow on the streets where cheap people live.

One evening when we were thus promenading, and I was trying to look like a prize St. Bernard, and the old man was trying to look like he wouldn't have murdered the first organ-grinder he heard play Mendelssohn's wedding-march, I looked up at him and said, in my way:

"What are you looking so sour about, you oakum trimmed lobster? She don't kiss you. You don't have to sit on her lap and listen to talk that would make the book of a musical comedy sound like the maxims of

Epictetus. You ought to be thankful you're not a dog. Brace up, Benedick, and bid the blues begone."

The matrimonial mishap looked down at me with almost canine intelligence in his face.

"Why, doggie," says he, "good doggie. You almost look like you could speak. What is it, doggie—Cats?"

Cats! Could speak!

But, of course, he couldn't understand. Humans were denied the speech of animals. The only common ground of communication upon which dogs and men can get together is in fiction.

In the flat across the hall from us lived a lady with a black-and-tan terrier. Her husband strung it and took it out every evening, but he always came home cheerful and whistling. One day I touched noses with the black-and-tan in the hall, and I struck him for an elucidation.

"See, here, Wiggle-and-Skip," I says, "you know that it ain't the nature of a real man to play dry nurse to a dog in public. I never saw one leashed to a bow-wow yet that didn't look like he'd like to lick every other man that looked at him. But your boss comes in every day as perky and set up as an amateur prestidigitator doing the egg trick. How does he do it? Don't tell me he likes it."

"Him?" says the black-and-tan. "Why, he uses Nature's Own Remedy. He gets spifflicated. At first when we go out he's as shy as the man on the steamer who would rather play pedro when they make 'em all jackpots. By the time we've been in eight saloons he don't care whether the thing on the end of his line is a dog or a catfish. I've lost two inches of my tail trying to sidestep those swinging doors."

The pointer I got from that terrier—vaudeville please copy—set me to thinking.

One evening about 6 o'clock my mistress ordered him to get busy and do the ozone act for Lovey. I have concealed it until now, but that is what she called me. The black-and-tan was called "Tweetness." I consider that I have the bulge on him as far as you could chase a rabbit. Still "Lovey" is something of a nomenclatural tin can on the tail of one's self respect.

At a quiet place on a safe street I tightened the line of my custodian in front of an attractive, refined saloon. I made a dead-ahead scramble for the doors, whining like a dog in the press despatches that lets the family know that little Alice is bogged while gathering lilies in the brook.

"Why, darn my eyes," says the old man, with a grin; "darn my eyes if the saffron-coloured son of a seltzer lemonade ain't asking me in to take a drink. Lemme see—how long's it been since I saved shoe leather by keeping one foot on the foot-rest? I believe I'll—"

I knew I had him. Hot Scotches he took, sitting at a table. For an hour he kept the Campbells coming. I sat by his side rapping for the waiter with my tail, and eating free lunch such as mamma in her flat never equalled with her homemade truck bought at a delicatessen store eight minutes before papa comes home.

When the products of Scotland were all exhausted except the rye bread the old man unwound me from the table leg and played me outside like a fisherman plays a salmon. Out there he took off my collar and threw it into the street.

"Poor doggie," says he; "good doggie. She shan't kiss you any more. 'S a darned shame. Good doggie, go away and get run over by a street car and be happy."

I refused to leave. I leaped and frisked around the old man's legs happy as a pug on a rug.

"You old flea-headed woodchuck-chaser," I said to him—"you moon-baying, rabbit-pointing, egg-stealing old beagle, can't you see that I don't want to leave you? Can't you see that we're both Pups in the Wood and the missis is the cruel uncle after you with the dish towel and me with the flea liniment and a pink bow to tie on my tail. Why not cut that all out and be pards forever more?"

Maybe you'll say he didn't understand—maybe he didn't. But he kind of got a grip on the Hot Scotches, and stood still for a minute, thinking.

"Doggie," says he, finally, "we don't live more than a dozen lives on this earth, and very few of us live to be more than 300. If I ever see that flat any more I'm a flat, and if you do you're flatter; and that's no flattery. I'm offering 60 to 1 that Westward Ho wins out by the length of a dachshund."

There was no string, but I frolicked along with my master to the Twenty-third street ferry. And the cats on the route saw reason to give thanks that prehensile claws had been given them.

On the Jersey side my master said to a stranger who stood eating a currant bun:

"Me and my doggie, we are bound for the Rocky Mountains."

But what pleased me most was when my old man pulled both of my ears until I howled, and said: "You common, monkey-headed, rat-tailed, sulphur-coloured son of a door mat, do you know what I'm going to call you?"

I thought of "Lovey," and I whined dolefully.

"I'm going to call you 'Pete,'" says my master; and if I'd had five tails I couldn't have done enough wagging to do justice to the occasion.

SPRINGTIME À LA CARTE

It was a day in March.

Never, never begin a story this way when you write one. No opening could possibly be worse. It is unimaginative, flat, dry and likely to consist of mere wind. But in this instance it is allowable. For the following paragraph, which should have inaugurated the narrative, is too wildly extravagant and preposterous to be flaunted in the face of the reader without preparation.

Sarah was crying over her bill of fare.

Think of a New York girl shedding tears on the menu card!

To account for this you will be allowed to guess that the lobsters were all out, or that she had sworn ice-cream off during Lent, or that she had ordered onions, or that she had just come from a Hackett matinee. And then, all these theories being wrong, you will please let the story proceed.

The gentleman who announced that the world was an oyster which he with his sword would open made a larger hit than he deserved. It is not difficult to open an oyster with a sword. But did you ever notice any one try to open the terrestrial bivalve with a typewriter? Like to wait for a dozen raw opened that way?

Sarah had managed to pry apart the shells with her unhandy weapon far enough to nibble a wee bit at the cold and clammy world within. She knew no more shorthand than if she had been a graduate in stenography just let slip upon the world by a business college. So, not being able to stenog, she could not enter that bright galaxy of office talent. She was a free-lance typewriter and canvassed for odd jobs of copying.

The most brilliant and crowning feat of Sarah's battle with the world was the deal she made with Schulenberg's Home Restaurant. The restaurant was next door to the old red brick in which she hall-roomed. One evening after dining at Schulenberg's 40-cent, five-course table d'hôte (served as fast as you throw the five baseballs at the coloured gentleman's head) Sarah took away with her the bill of fare. It was written in an almost unreadable script neither English nor German, and so arranged that if you were not careful you began with a toothpick and rice pudding and ended with soup and the day of the week.

The next day Sarah showed Schulenberg a neat card on which the menu was beautifully typewritten with the viands temptingly marshalled under their right and proper heads from "hors d'oeuvre" to "not responsible for overcoats and umbrellas."

Schulenberg became a naturalised citizen on the spot. Before Sarah left him she had him willingly committed to an agreement. She was to furnish typewritten bills of fare for the twenty-one tables in the restaurant—a new bill for each day's dinner, and new ones for breakfast and lunch as often as changes occurred in the food or as neatness required.

In return for this Schulenberg was to send three meals per diem to Sarah's hall room by a waiter—an obsequious one if possible—and furnish her each afternoon with a pencil draft of what Fate had in store for Schulenberg's customers on the morrow.

Mutual satisfaction resulted from the agreement. Schulenberg's patrons now knew what the food they ate was called even if its nature sometimes puzzled them. And Sarah had food during a cold, dull winter, which was the main thing with her.

And then the almanac lied, and said that spring had come. Spring comes when it comes. The frozen snows of January still lay like adamant in the crosstown streets. The hand-organs still played "In the Good Old Summertime," with their December vivacity and expression. Men began to make thirty-day notes to buy Easter dresses. Janitors shut off steam. And when these things happen one may know that the city is still in the clutches of winter.

One afternoon Sarah shivered in her elegant hall bedroom; "house heated; scrupulously clean; conveniences; seen to be appreciated." She had no work to do except Schulenberg's menu cards. Sarah sat in her squeaky willow rocker, and looked out the window. The calendar on the wall kept crying to her: "Springtime is here, Sarah—springtime is here, I tell you. Look at me, Sarah, my figures show it. You've got a neat figure yourself, Sarah—a—nice springtime figure—why do you look out the window so sadly?"

Sarah's room was at the back of the house. Looking out the window she could see the windowless rear brick wall of the box factory on the next street. But the wall was clearest crystal; and Sarah was looking down a grassy lane shaded with cherry trees and elms and bordered with raspberry bushes and Cherokee roses.

Spring's real harbingers are too subtle for the eye and ear. Some must have the flowering crocus, the wood-starring dogwood, the voice of bluebird—even so gross a reminder as the farewell handshake of the retiring buckwheat and oyster before they can welcome the Lady in Green to their dull bosoms. But to old earth's choicest kin there come straight, sweet messages from his newest bride, telling them they shall be no stepchildren unless they choose to be.

On the previous summer Sarah had gone into the country and loved a farmer.

(In writing your story never hark back thus. It is bad art, and cripples interest. Let it march, march.)

Sarah stayed two weeks at Sunnybrook Farm. There she learned to love old Farmer Franklin's son Walter. Farmers have been loved and wedded and turned out to grass in less time. But young Walter Franklin was a modern agriculturist. He had a telephone in his cow house, and he could figure up exactly what effect next year's Canada wheat crop would have on potatoes planted in the dark of the moon.

It was in this shaded and raspberried lane that Walter had wooed and won her. And together they had sat and woven a crown of dandelions for her hair. He had immoderately praised the effect of the yellow blossoms against her brown tresses; and she had left the chaplet there, and walked back to the house swinging her straw sailor in her hands.

They were to marry in the spring—at the very first signs of spring, Walter said. And Sarah came back to the city to pound her typewriter.

A knock at the door dispelled Sarah's visions of that happy day. A waiter had brought the rough pencil draft of the Home Restaurant's next day fare in old Schulenberg's angular hand.

Sarah sat down to her typewriter and slipped a card between the rollers. She was a nimble worker. Generally in an hour and a half the twenty-one menu cards were written and ready.

To-day there were more changes on the bill of fare than usual. The soups were lighter; pork was eliminated from the entrées, figuring only with Russian turnips among the roasts. The gracious spirit of spring pervaded the entire menu. Lamb, that lately capered on the greening hillsides, was becoming exploited with the sauce that commemorated its gambols. The song of the oyster, though not silenced, was dimuendo con amore. The frying-pan seemed to be held, inactive, behind the beneficent bars of the broiler. The pie list swelled; the richer puddings had vanished; the sausage, with his drapery wrapped about him, barely lingered in a pleasant thanatopsis with the buckwheats and the sweet but doomed maple.

Sarah's fingers danced like midgets above a summer stream. Down through the courses she worked, giving each item its position according to its length with an accurate eye. Just above the desserts came the list of vegetables. Carrots and peas, asparagus on toast, the perennial tomatoes and corn and succotash, lima beans, cabbage—and then—

Sarah was crying over her bill of fare. Tears from the depths of some divine despair rose in her heart and gathered to her eyes. Down went her head on the little typewriter stand; and the keyboard rattled a dry accompaniment to her moist sobs.

For she had received no letter from Walter in two weeks, and the next item on the bill of fare was dandelions—dandelions with some kind of egg—but bother the egg!—dandelions, with whose golden blooms Walter had crowned her his queen of love and future bride—dandelions, the harbingers of spring, her sorrow's crown of sorrow—reminder of her happiest days.

Madam, I dare you to smile until you suffer this test: Let the Marechal Niel roses that Percy brought you on the night you gave him your heart be served as a salad with French dressing before your eyes at a Schulenberg table d'hôte. Had Juliet so seen her love tokens dishonoured the sooner would she have sought the lethean herbs of the good apothecary.

But what a witch is Spring! Into the great cold city of stone and iron a message had to be sent. There was none to convey it but the little hardy courier of the fields with his rough green coat and modest air. He is a true soldier of fortune, this dent-de-lion—this lion's tooth, as the French chefs call him. Flowered, he will assist at love-making, wreathed in my lady's nut-brown hair; young and callow and unblossomed, he goes into the boiling pot and delivers the word of his sovereign mistress.

By and by Sarah forced back her tears. The cards must be written. But, still in a faint, golden glow from her dandeleonine dream, she fingered the typewriter keys absently for a little while, with her mind and heart in the meadow lane with her young farmer. But soon she came swiftly back to the rock-bound lanes of Manhattan, and the typewriter began to rattle and jump like a strike-breaker's motor car.

At 6 o'clock the waiter brought her dinner and carried away the typewritten bill of fare. When Sarah ate she set aside, with a sigh, the dish of dandelions with its crowning ovarious accompaniment. As this dark mass had been transformed from a bright and love-indorsed flower to be an ignominious vegetable, so had her summer hopes wilted and perished. Love may, as Shakespeare said, feed on itself: but Sarah could not bring herself to eat the dandelions that had graced, as ornaments, the first spiritual banquet of her heart's true affection.

At 7:30 the couple in the next room began to quarrel: the man in the room above sought for A on his flute; the gas went a little lower; three coal wagons started to unload—the only sound of which the phonograph is jealous; cats on the back fences slowly retreated toward Mukden. By these signs Sarah knew that it was time for her to read. She got out "The Cloister and the Hearth," the best non-selling book of the month, settled her feet on her trunk, and began to wander with Gerard.

The front door bell rang. The landlady answered it. Sarah left Gerard and Denys treed by a bear and listened. Oh, yes; you would, just as she did!

And then a strong voice was heard in the hall below, and Sarah jumped for her door, leaving the book on the floor and the first round easily the bear's. You have guessed it. She reached the top of the stairs just as her farmer came up, three at a jump, and reaped and garnered her, with nothing left for the gleaners.

"Why haven't you written—oh, why?" cried Sarah.

"New York is a pretty large town," said Walter Franklin. "I came in a week ago to your old address. I found that you went away on a Thursday. That consoled some; it eliminated the possible Friday bad luck. But it didn't prevent my hunting for you with police and otherwise ever since!

"I wrote!" said Sarah, vehemently.

"Never got it!"

"Then how did you find me?"

The young farmer smiled a springtime smile.

"I dropped into that Home Restaurant next door this evening," said he. "I don't care who knows it; I like a dish of some kind of greens at this time of the year. I ran my eye down that nice typewritten bill of fare looking for something in that line. When I got below cabbage I turned my chair over and hollered for the proprietor. He told me where you lived."

"I remember," sighed Sarah, happily. "That was dandelions below cabbage."

"I'd know that cranky capital W way above the line that your typewriter makes anywhere in the world," said Franklin.

"Why, there's no W in dandelions," said Sarah, in surprise.

The young man drew the bill of fare from his pocket, and pointed to a line.

Sarah recognised the first card she had typewritten that afternoon. There was still the rayed splotch in the upper right-hand corner where a tear had fallen. But over the spot where one should have read the name of the meadow plant, the clinging memory of their golden blossoms had allowed her fingers to strike strange keys.

Between the red cabbage and the stuffed green peppers was the item:

"DEAREST WALTER, WITH HARD-BOILED EGG."

BETWEEN ROUNDS

The May moon shone bright upon the private boarding-house of Mrs. Murphy. By reference to the almanac a large amount of territory will be discovered upon which its rays also fell. Spring was in its heydey, with hay fever soon to follow. The parks were green with new leaves and buyers for the Western and Southern trade. Flowers and summer-resort agents were blowing; the air and answers to Lawson were growing milder; hand-organs, fountains and pinochle were playing everywhere.

The windows of Mrs. Murphy's boarding-house were open. A group of boarders were seated on the high stoop upon round, flat mats like German pancakes.

In one of the second-floor front windows Mrs. McCaskey awaited her husband. Supper was cooling on the table. Its heat went into Mrs. McCaskey.

At nine Mr. McCaskey came. He carried his coat on his arm and his pipe in his teeth; and he apologised for disturbing the boarders on the steps as he selected spots of stone between them on which to set his size 9, width Ds.

As he opened the door of his room he received a surprise. Instead of the usual stove-lid or potato-masher for him to dodge, came only words.

Mr. McCaskey reckoned that the benign May moon had softened the breast of his spouse.

"I heard ye," came the oral substitutes for kitchenware. "Ye can apollygise to riff-raff of the streets for settin' yer unhandy feet on the tails of their frocks, but ye'd walk on the neck of yer wife the length of a clothes-line without so much as a 'Kiss me fut,' and I'm sure it's that long from rubberin' out the windy for ye and the victuals cold such as there's money to buy after drinkin' up yer wages at Gallegher's every Saturday evenin', and the gas man here twice to-day for his."

"Woman!" said Mr. McCaskey, dashing his coat and hat upon a chair, "the noise of ye is an insult to me appetite. When ye run down politeness ye take the mortar from between the bricks of the foundations of society. 'Tis no more than exercisin' the acrimony of a gentleman when ye ask the dissent of ladies blockin' the way for steppin' between them. Will ye bring the pig's face of ye out of the windy and see to the food?"

Mrs. McCaskey arose heavily and went to the stove. There was something in her manner that warned Mr. McCaskey. When the corners of her mouth went down suddenly like a barometer it usually foretold a fall of crockery and tinware.

"Pig's face, is it?" said Mrs. McCaskey, and hurled a stewpan full of bacon and turnips at her lord.

Mr. McCaskey was no novice at repartee. He knew what should follow the entrée. On the table was a roast sirloin of pork, garnished with shamrocks. He retorted with this, and drew the appropriate return of a bread pudding in an earthen dish. A hunk of Swiss cheese accurately thrown by her husband struck Mrs. McCaskey below one eye. When she replied with a well-aimed coffee-pot full of a hot, black, semi-fragrant liquid the battle, according to courses, should have ended.

But Mr. McCaskey was no 50-cent table d'hôter. Let cheap Bohemians consider coffee the end, if they would. Let them make that faux pas. He was foxier still. Finger-bowls were not beyond the compass of his experience. They were not to be had in the Pension Murphy; but their equivalent was at hand. Triumphantly he sent the granite-ware wash basin at the head of his matrimonial adversary. Mrs. McCaskey dodged in time. She reached for a flatiron, with which, as a sort of cordial, she hoped to bring the gastronomical duel to a close. But a loud, wailing scream downstairs caused both her and Mr. McCaskey to pause in a sort of involuntary armistice.

On the sidewalk at the corner of the house Policeman Cleary was standing with one ear upturned, listening to the crash of household utensils.

"'Tis Jawn McCaskey and his missis at it again," meditated the policeman. "I wonder shall I go up and stop the row. I will not. Married folks they are; and few pleasures they have. 'Twill not last long. Sure, they'll have to borrow more dishes to keep it up with."

And just then came the loud scream below-stairs, betokening fear or dire extremity. "'Tis probably the cat," said Policeman Cleary, and walked hastily in the other direction.

The boarders on the steps were fluttered. Mr. Toomey, an insurance solicitor by birth and an investigator by profession, went inside to analyse the scream. He returned with the news that Mrs. Murphy's little boy, Mike, was lost. Following the messenger, out bounced Mrs. Murphy—two hundred pounds in tears and hysterics, clutching the air and howling to the sky for the loss of thirty pounds of freckles and mischief. Bathos, truly; but Mr. Toomey sat down at the side of Miss Purdy, millinery, and their hands came together in sympathy. The two old maids, Misses Walsh, who complained every day about the noise in the halls, inquired immediately if anybody had looked behind the clock.

Major Grigg, who sat by his fat wife on the top step, arose and buttoned his coat. "The little one lost?" he exclaimed. "I will scour the city." His wife never allowed him out after dark. But now she said: "Go, Ludovic!" in a baritone voice. "Whoever can look upon that mother's grief without springing to her relief has a heart of stone." "Give me some thirty or—sixty cents, my love," said the Major. "Lost children sometimes stray far. I may need carfares."

Old man Denny, hall room, fourth floor back, who sat on the lowest step, trying to read a paper by the street lamp, turned over a page to follow up the article about the carpenters' strike. Mrs. Murphy shrieked to the moon: "Oh, ar-r-Mike, f'r Gawd's sake, where is me little bit av a boy?"

"When'd ye see him last?" asked old man Denny, with one eye on the report of the Building Trades League.

"Oh," wailed Mrs. Murphy, "'twas yisterday, or maybe four hours ago! I dunno. But it's lost he is, me little boy Mike. He was playin' on the sidewalk only this mornin'—or was it Wednesday? I'm that busy with work, 'tis hard to keep up with dates. But I've looked the house over from top to cellar, and it's gone he is. Oh, for the love av Hiven—"

Silent, grim, colossal, the big city has ever stood against its revilers. They call it hard as iron; they say that no pulse of pity beats in its bosom; they compare its streets with lonely forests and deserts of lava. But beneath the hard crust of the lobster is found a delectable and luscious food. Perhaps a different simile would have been wiser. Still, nobody should take offence. We would call no one a lobster without good and sufficient claws.

No calamity so touches the common heart of humanity as does the straying of a little child. Their feet are so uncertain and feeble; the ways are so steep and strange.

Major Griggs hurried down to the corner, and up the avenue into Billy's place. "Gimme a rye-high," he said to the servitor. "Haven't seen a bow-legged, dirty-faced little devil of a six-year-old lost kid around here anywhere, have you?"

Mr. Toomey retained Miss Purdy's hand on the steps. "Think of that dear little babe," said Miss Purdy, "lost from his mother's side— perhaps already fallen beneath the iron hoofs of galloping steeds—oh, isn't it dreadful?"

"Ain't that right?" agreed Mr. Toomey, squeezing her hand. "Say I start out and help look for um!"

"Perhaps," said Miss Purdy, "you should. But, oh, Mr. Toomey, you are so dashing—so reckless—suppose in your enthusiasm some accident should befall you, then what—"

Old man Denny read on about the arbitration agreement, with one finger on the lines.

In the second floor front Mr. and Mrs. McCaskey came to the window to recover their second wind. Mr. McCaskey was scooping turnips out of his vest with a crooked forefinger, and his lady was wiping an eye that the salt of the roast pork had not benefited. They heard the outcry below, and thrust their heads out of the window.

"'Tis little Mike is lost," said Mrs. McCaskey, in a hushed voice, "the beautiful, little, trouble-making angel of a gossoon!"

"The bit of a boy mislaid?" said Mr. McCaskey, leaning out of the window. "Why, now, that's bad enough, entirely. The childer, they be different. If 'twas a woman I'd be willin', for they leave peace behind 'em when they go."

Disregarding the thrust, Mrs. McCaskey caught her husband's arm.

"Jawn," she said, sentimentally, "Missis Murphy's little bye is lost. 'Tis a great city for losing little boys. Six years old he was. Jawn, 'tis the same age our little bye would have been if we had had one six years ago."

"We never did," said Mr. McCaskey, lingering with the fact.

"But if we had, Jawn, think what sorrow would be in our hearts this night, with our little Phelan run away and stolen in the city nowheres at all."

"Ye talk foolishness," said Mr. McCaskey. "'Tis Pat he would be named, after me old father in Cantrim."

"Ye lie!" said Mrs. McCaskey, without anger. "Me brother was worth tin dozen bog-trotting McCaskeys. After him would the bye be named." She leaned over the window-sill and looked down at the hurrying and bustle below.

"Jawn," said Mrs. McCaskey, softly, "I'm sorry I was hasty wid ye."

"'Twas hasty puddin', as ye say," said her husband, "and hurry-up turnips and get-a-move-on-ye coffee. 'Twas what ye could call a quick lunch, all right, and tell no lie."

Mrs. McCaskey slipped her arm inside her husband's and took his rough hand in hers.

"Listen at the cryin' of poor Mrs. Murphy," she said. "'Tis an awful thing for a bit of a bye to be lost in this great big city. If 'twas our little Phelan, Jawn, I'd be breakin' me heart."

Awkwardly Mr. McCaskey withdrew his hand. But he laid it around the nearing shoulder of his wife.

"'Tis foolishness, of course," said he, roughly, "but I'd be cut up some meself if our little Pat was kidnapped or anything. But there never was any childer for us. Sometimes I've been ugly and hard with ye, Judy. Forget it."

They leaned together, and looked down at the heart-drama being acted below.

Long they sat thus. People surged along the sidewalk, crowding, questioning, filling the air with rumours, and inconsequent surmises. Mrs. Murphy ploughed back and forth in their midst, like a soft mountain down which plunged an audible cataract of tears. Couriers came and went.

Loud voices and a renewed uproar were raised in front of the boarding-house.

"What's up now, Judy?" asked Mr. McCaskey.

"'Tis Missis Murphy's voice," said Mrs. McCaskey, harking. "She says she's after finding little Mike asleep behind the roll of old linoleum under the bed in her room."

Mr. McCaskey laughed loudly.

"That's yer Phelan," he shouted, sardonically. "Divil a bit would a Pat have done that trick. If the bye we never had is strayed and stole, by the powers, call him Phelan, and see him hide out under the bed like a mangy pup."

Mrs. McCaskey arose heavily, and went toward the dish closet, with the corners of her mouth drawn down.

Policeman Cleary came back around the corner as the crowd dispersed. Surprised, he upturned an ear toward the McCaskey apartment, where the crash of irons and chinaware and the ring of

99

hurled kitchen utensils seemed as loud as before. Policeman Cleary took out his timepiece.

"By the deported snakes!" he exclaimed, "Jawn McCaskey and his lady have been fightin' for an hour and a quarter by the watch. The missis could give him forty pounds weight. Strength to his arm."

Policeman Cleary strolled back around the corner.

Old man Denny folded his paper and hurried up the steps just as Mrs. Murphy was about to lock the door for the night.

THE GIFT OF THE MAGI

One dollar and eighty-seven cents. That was all. And sixty cents of it was in pennies. Pennies saved one and two at a time by bulldozing the grocer and the vegetable man and the butcher until one's cheeks burned with the silent imputation of parsimony that such close dealing implied. Three times Della counted it. One dollar and eighty-seven cents. And the next day would be Christmas.

There was clearly nothing to do but flop down on the shabby little couch and howl. So Della did it. Which instigates the moral reflection that life is made up of sobs, sniffles, and smiles, with sniffles predominating.

While the mistress of the home is gradually subsiding from the first stage to the second, take a look at the home. A furnished flat at $8 per week. It did not exactly beggar description, but it certainly had that word on the lookout for the mendicancy squad.

In the vestibule below was a letter-box into which no letter would go, and an electric button from which no mortal finger could coax a ring. Also appertaining thereunto was a card bearing the name "Mr. James Dillingham Young." The "Dillingham" had been flung to the breeze during a former period of prosperity when its possessor was being paid $30 per week. Now, when the income was shrunk to $20, the letters of "Dillingham" looked blurred, as though they were thinking seriously of contracting to a modest and unassuming D. But whenever Mr. James Dillingham Young came home and reached his flat above he was called "Jim" and greatly hugged by Mrs. James Dillingham Young, already introduced to you as Della. Which is all very good.

Della finished her cry and attended to her cheeks with the powder rag. She stood by the window and looked out dully at a grey cat walking a grey fence in a grey backyard. Tomorrow would be Christmas Day, and she had only $1.87 with which to buy Jim a present. She had been saving every penny she could for months, with this result. Twenty dollars a week doesn't go far. Expenses had been greater than she had calculated. They always are. Only $1.87 to buy a present for Jim. Her Jim. Many a happy hour she had spent planning for something nice for him. Something fine and rare and sterling—something just a little bit near to being worthy of the honour of being owned by Jim.

There was a pier-glass between the windows of the room. Perhaps you have seen a pier-glass in an $8 flat. A very thin and very agile person may, by observing his reflection in a rapid sequence of longitudinal strips, obtain a fairly accurate conception of his looks. Della, being slender, had mastered the art.

Suddenly she whirled from the window and stood before the glass. Her eyes were shining brilliantly, but her face had lost its colour within twenty seconds. Rapidly she pulled down her hair and let it fall to its full length.

Now, there were two possessions of the James Dillingham Youngs in which they both took a mighty pride. One was Jim's gold watch that had been his father's and his grandfather's. The other was Della's hair.

Had the Queen of Sheba lived in the flat across the airshaft, Della would have let her hair hang out the window some day to dry just to depreciate Her Majesty's jewels and gifts. Had King Solomon been the janitor, with all his treasures piled up in the basement, Jim would have pulled out his watch every time he passed, just to see him pluck at his beard from envy.

So now Della's beautiful hair fell about her, rippling and shining like a cascade of brown waters. It reached below her knee and made itself almost a garment for her. And then she did it up again nervously and quickly. Once she faltered for a minute and stood still while a tear or two splashed on the worn red carpet.

On went her old brown jacket; on went her old brown hat. With a whirl of skirts and with the brilliant sparkle still in her eyes, she fluttered out the door and down the stairs to the street.

Where she stopped the sign read: "Mme. Sofronie. Hair Goods of All Kinds." One flight up Della ran, and collected herself, panting. Madame, large, too white, chilly, hardly looked the "Sofronie."

"Will you buy my hair?" asked Della.

"I buy hair," said Madame. "Take yer hat off and let's have a sight at the looks of it."

Down rippled the brown cascade. "Twenty dollars," said Madame, lifting the mass with a practised hand.

"Give it to me quick," said Della.

Oh, and the next two hours tripped by on rosy wings. Forget the hashed metaphor. She was ransacking the stores for Jim's present.

She found it at last. It surely had been made for Jim and no one else. There was no other like it in any of the stores, and she had turned all of them inside out. It was a platinum fob chain simple and chaste in design, properly proclaiming its value by substance alone and not by meretricious ornamentation—as all good things should do. It was even worthy of The Watch. As soon as she saw it she knew that it must be Jim's. It was like him. Quietness and value—the description applied to both. Twenty-one dollars they took from her for it, and she hurried home with the 87 cents. With that chain on his watch Jim might be properly anxious about the time in any company. Grand as the watch was, he sometimes looked at it on the sly on account of the old leather strap that he used in place of a chain.

When Della reached home her intoxication gave way a little to prudence and reason. She got out her curling irons and lighted the gas and went to work repairing the ravages made by generosity added to love. Which is always a tremendous task, dear friends—a mammoth task.

Within forty minutes her head was covered with tiny, close-lying curls that made her look wonderfully like a truant schoolboy. She looked at her reflection in the mirror long, carefully, and critically.

"If Jim doesn't kill me," she said to herself, "before he takes a second look at me, he'll say I look like a Coney Island chorus girl. But what could I do—oh! what could I do with a dollar and eighty-seven cents?"

At 7 o'clock the coffee was made and the frying-pan was on the back of the stove hot and ready to cook the chops.

Jim was never late. Della doubled the fob chain in her hand and sat on the corner of the table near the door that he always entered. Then she heard his step on the stair away down on the first flight, and she turned white for just a moment. She had a habit for saying little silent prayers about the simplest everyday things, and now she whispered: "Please God, make him think I am still pretty."

The door opened and Jim stepped in and closed it. He looked thin and very serious. Poor fellow, he was only twenty-two—and to be burdened with a family! He needed a new overcoat and he was without gloves.

Jim stopped inside the door, as immovable as a setter at the scent of quail. His eyes were fixed upon Della, and there was an expression in them that she could not read, and it terrified her. It was not anger, nor surprise, nor disapproval, nor horror, nor any of the sentiments that she had been prepared for. He simply stared at her fixedly with that peculiar expression on his face.

Della wriggled off the table and went for him.

"Jim, darling," she cried, "don't look at me that way. I had my hair cut off and sold because I couldn't have lived through Christmas without giving you a present. It'll grow out again—you won't mind, will you? I just had to do it. My hair grows awfully fast. Say 'Merry Christmas!' Jim, and let's be happy. You don't know what a nice—what a beautiful, nice gift I've got for you."

"You've cut off your hair?" asked Jim, laboriously, as if he had not arrived at that patent fact yet even after the hardest mental labor.

"Cut it off and sold it," said Della. "Don't you like me just as well, anyhow? I'm me without my hair, ain't I?"

Jim looked about the room curiously.

"You say your hair is gone?" he said, with an air almost of idiocy.

"You needn't look for it," said Della. "It's sold, I tell you—sold and gone, too. It's Christmas Eve, boy. Be good to me, for it went for you. Maybe the hairs of my head were numbered," she went on with sudden serious sweetness, "but nobody could ever count my love for you. Shall I put the chops on, Jim?"

Out of his trance Jim seemed quickly to wake. He enfolded his Della. For ten seconds let us regard with discreet scrutiny some inconsequential object in the other direction. Eight dollars a week or a million a year—what is the difference? A mathematician or a wit would give you the wrong answer. The magi brought valuable gifts, but that was not among them. This dark assertion will be illuminated later on.

Jim drew a package from his overcoat pocket and threw it upon the table.

"Don't make any mistake, Dell," he said, "about me. I don't think there's anything in the way of a haircut or a shave or a shampoo that could make me like my girl any less. But if you'll unwrap that package you may see why you had me going a while at first."

White fingers and nimble tore at the string and paper. And then an ecstatic scream of joy; and then, alas! a quick feminine change to hysterical tears and wails, necessitating the immediate employment of all the comforting powers of the lord of the flat.

For there lay The Combs—the set of combs, side and back, that Della had worshipped long in a Broadway window. Beautiful combs, pure tortoise shell, with jewelled rims—just the shade to wear in the beautiful vanished hair. They were expensive combs, she knew, and her heart had simply craved and yearned over them without the least hope of possession. And now, they were hers, but the tresses that should have adorned the coveted adornments were gone.

But she hugged them to her bosom, and at length she was able to look up with dim eyes and a smile and say: "My hair grows so fast, Jim!"

And then Della leaped up like a little singed cat and cried, "Oh, oh!"

Jim had not yet seen his beautiful present. She held it out to him eagerly upon her open palm. The dull precious metal seemed to flash with a reflection of her bright and ardent spirit.

"Isn't it a dandy, Jim? I hunted all over town to find it. You'll have to look at the time a hundred times a day now. Give me your watch. I want to see how it looks on it."

Instead of obeying, Jim tumbled down on the couch and put his hands under the back of his head and smiled.

"Dell," said he, "let's put our Christmas presents away and keep 'em a while. They're too nice to use just at present. I sold the watch to get the money to buy your combs. And now suppose you put the chops on."

The magi, as you know, were wise men—wonderfully wise men—who brought gifts to the Babe in the manger. They invented the art of giving Christmas presents. Being wise, their gifts were no doubt wise ones, possibly bearing the privilege of exchange in case of duplication. And here I have lamely related to you the uneventful chronicle of two foolish children in a flat who most unwisely sacrificed for each other the greatest treasures of their house. But in a last word to the wise of these days let it be said that of all who give gifts these two were the wisest. Of all who give and receive gifts, such as they are wisest. Everywhere they are wisest. They are the magi.

THE LOVE-PHILTRE OF IKEY SCHOENSTEIN

The Blue Light Drug Store is downtown, between the Bowery and First Avenue, where the distance between the two streets is the shortest. The Blue Light does not consider that pharmacy is a thing of bric-a-brac, scent and ice-cream soda. If you ask it for pain-killer it will not give you a bonbon.

The Blue Light scorns the labour-saving arts of modern pharmacy. It macerates its opium and percolates its own laudanum and paregoric. To this day pills are made behind its tall prescription desk—pills rolled out on its own pill-tile, divided with a spatula, rolled with the finger and thumb, dusted with calcined magnesia and delivered in little round pasteboard pill-boxes. The store is on a corner about which coveys of ragged-plumed, hilarious children play and become candidates for the cough drops and soothing syrups that wait for them inside.

Ikey Schoenstein was the night clerk of the Blue Light and the friend of his customers. Thus it is on the East Side, where the heart of pharmacy is not glacé. There, as it should be, the druggist is a counsellor, a confessor, an adviser, an able and willing missionary and mentor whose learning is respected, whose occult wisdom is venerated and whose medicine is often poured, untasted, into the gutter. Therefore Ikey's corniform, be-spectacled nose and narrow, knowledge-bowed figure was well known in the vicinity of the Blue Light, and his advice and notice were much desired.

Ikey roomed and breakfasted at Mrs. Riddle's two squares away. Mrs. Riddle had a daughter named Rosy. The circumlocution has been in vain—you must have guessed it—Ikey adored Rosy. She tinctured all his thoughts; she was the compound extract of all that was chemically pure and officinal—the dispensatory contained nothing equal to her. But Ikey was timid, and his hopes remained insoluble in the menstruum of his backwardness and fears. Behind his counter he was a superior being, calmly conscious of special knowledge and worth; outside he was a weak-kneed, purblind, motorman-cursed rambler, with ill-fitting clothes stained with chemicals and smelling of socotrine aloes and valerianate of ammonia.

The fly in Ikey's ointment (thrice welcome, pat trope!) was Chunk McGowan.

Mr. McGowan was also striving to catch the bright smiles tossed about by Rosy. But he was no outfielder as Ikey was; he picked them off the bat. At the same time he was Ikey's friend and customer, and often dropped in at the Blue Light Drug Store to have a bruise painted with iodine or get a cut rubber-plastered after a pleasant evening spent along the Bowery.

One afternoon McGowan drifted in in his silent, easy way, and sat, comely, smooth-faced, hard, indomitable, good-natured, upon a stool.

"Ikey," said he, when his friend had fetched his mortar and sat opposite, grinding gum benzoin to a powder, "get busy with your ear. It's drugs for me if you've got the line I need."

Ikey scanned the countenance of Mr. McGowan for the usual evidences of conflict, but found none.

"Take your coat off," he ordered. "I guess already that you have been stuck in the ribs with a knife. I have many times told you those Dagoes would do you up."

Mr. McGowan smiled. "Not them," he said. "Not any Dagoes. But you've located the diagnosis all right enough—it's under my coat, near the ribs. Say! Ikey—Rosy and me are goin' to run away and get married to-night."

Ikey's left forefinger was doubled over the edge of the mortar, holding it steady. He gave it a wild rap with the pestle, but felt it not. Meanwhile Mr. McGowan's smile faded to a look of perplexed gloom.

"That is," he continued, "if she keeps in the notion until the time comes. We've been layin' pipes for the getaway for two weeks. One day she says she will; the same evenin' she says nixy. We've agreed on to-night, and Rosy's stuck to the affirmative this time for two whole days. But it's five hours yet till the time, and I'm afraid she'll stand me up when it comes to the scratch."

"You said you wanted drugs," remarked Ikey.

Mr. McGowan looked ill at ease and harassed—a condition opposed to his usual line of demeanour. He made a patent-medicine almanac into a roll and fitted it with unprofitable carefulness about his finger.

"I wouldn't have this double handicap make a false start to-night for a million," he said. "I've got a little flat up in Harlem all ready, with chrysanthemums on the table and a kettle ready to boil. And I've engaged a pulpit pounder to be ready at his house for us at 9.30. It's got to come off. And if Rosy don't change her mind again!"—Mr. McGowan ceased, a prey to his doubts.

"I don't see then yet," said Ikey, shortly, "what makes it that you talk of drugs, or what I can be doing about it."

"Old man Riddle don't like me a little bit," went on the uneasy suitor, bent upon marshalling his arguments. "For a week he hasn't let Rosy step outside the door with me. If it wasn't for losin' a boarder they'd have bounced me long ago. I'm makin' $20 a week and she'll never regret flyin' the coop with Chunk McGowan."

"You will excuse me, Chunk," said Ikey. "I must make a prescription that is to be called for soon."

"Say," said McGowan, looking up suddenly, "say, Ikey, ain't there a drug of some kind—some kind of powders that'll make a girl like you better if you give 'em to her?"

Ikey's lip beneath his nose curled with the scorn of superior enlightenment; but before he could answer, McGowan continued:

"Tim Lacy told me he got some once from a croaker uptown and fed 'em to his girl in soda water. From the very first dose he was ace-high and everybody else looked like thirty cents to her. They was married in less than two weeks."

Strong and simple was Chunk McGowan. A better reader of men than Ikey was could have seen that his tough frame was strung upon fine wires. Like a good general who was about to invade the enemy's territory he was seeking to guard every point against possible failure.

"I thought," went on Chunk hopefully, "that if I had one of them powders to give Rosy when I see her at supper to-night it might brace her up and keep her from reneging on the proposition to skip. I guess she don't need a mule team to drag her away, but women are better at coaching than they are at running bases. If the stuff'll work just for a couple of hours it'll do the trick."

"When is this foolishness of running away to be happening?" asked Ikey.

"Nine o'clock," said Mr. McGowan. "Supper's at seven. At eight Rosy goes to bed with a headache. At nine old Parvenzano lets me through to his back yard, where there's a board off Riddle's fence, next door. I go under her window and help her down the fire-escape. We've got to make it early on the preacher's account. It's all dead easy if Rosy don't balk when the flag drops. Can you fix me one of them powders, Ikey?"

Ikey Schoenstein rubbed his nose slowly.

"Chunk," said he, "it is of drugs of that nature that pharmaceutists must have much carefulness. To you alone of my acquaintance would I intrust a powder like that. But for you I shall make it, and you shall see how it makes Rosy to think of you."

Ikey went behind the prescription desk. There he crushed to a powder two soluble tablets, each containing a quarter of a grain of morphia.

To them he added a little sugar of milk to increase the bulk, and folded the mixture neatly in a white paper. Taken by an adult this powder would insure several hours of heavy slumber without danger to the sleeper. This he handed to Chunk McGowan, telling him to administer it in a liquid if possible, and received the hearty thanks of the backyard Lochinvar.

The subtlety of Ikey's action becomes apparent upon recital of his subsequent move. He sent a messenger for Mr. Riddle and disclosed the plans of Mr. McGowan for eloping with Rosy. Mr. Riddle was a stout man, brick-dusty of complexion and sudden in action.

"Much obliged," he said, briefly, to Ikey. "The lazy Irish loafer! My own room's just above Rosy's. I'll just go up there myself after supper and load the shot-gun and wait. If he comes in my back yard he'll go away in a ambulance instead of a bridal chaise."

With Rosy held in the clutches of Morpheus for a many-hours deep slumber, and the bloodthirsty parent waiting, armed and forewarned, Ikey felt that his rival was close, indeed, upon discomfiture.

All night in the Blue Light Drug Store he waited at his duties for chance news of the tragedy, but none came.

At eight o'clock in the morning the day clerk arrived and Ikey started hurriedly for Mrs. Riddle's to learn the outcome. And, lo! as he stepped out of the store who but Chunk McGowan sprang from a passing street car and grasped his hand—Chunk McGowan with a victor's smile and flushed with joy.

"Pulled it off," said Chunk with Elysium in his grin. "Rosy hit the fire-escape on time to a second, and we was under the wire at the Reverend's at 9.30 ¼. She's up at the flat—she cooked eggs this mornin' in a blue kimono—Lord! how lucky I am! You must pace up some day, Ikey, and feed with us. I've got a job down near the bridge, and that's where I'm heading for now."

"The—the—powder?" stammered Ikey.

"Oh, that stuff you gave me!" said Chunk, broadening his grin; "well, it was this way. I sat down at the supper table last night at Riddle's, and I looked at Rosy, and I says to myself, 'Chunk, if you get the girl get her on the square—don't try any hocus-pocus with a thoroughbred like her.' And I keeps the paper you give me in my pocket. And then my lamps fall on another party present, who, I says to myself, is failin' in a proper affection toward his comin' son-in-law, so I watches my chance and dumps that powder in old man Riddle's coffee—see?"

AFTER TWENTY YEARS

The policeman on the beat moved up the avenue impressively. The impressiveness was habitual and not for show, for spectators were few. The time was barely 10 o'clock at night, but chilly gusts of wind with a taste of rain in them had well nigh de-peopled the streets.

Trying doors as he went, twirling his club with many intricate and artful movements, turning now and then to cast his watchful eye adown the pacific thoroughfare, the officer, with his stalwart form and slight swagger, made a fine picture of a guardian of the peace. The vicinity was one that kept early hours. Now and then you might see the lights of a cigar store or of an all-night lunch counter; but the majority of the doors belonged to business places that had long since been closed.

When about midway of a certain block the policeman suddenly slowed his walk. In the doorway of a darkened hardware store a man leaned, with an unlighted cigar in his mouth. As the policeman walked up to him the man spoke up quickly.

"It's all right, officer," he said, reassuringly. "I'm just waiting for a friend. It's an appointment made twenty years ago. Sounds a little funny to you, doesn't it? Well, I'll explain if you'd like to make certain it's all straight. About that long ago there used to be a restaurant where this store stands—'Big Joe' Brady's restaurant."

"Until five years ago," said the policeman. "It was torn down then."

The man in the doorway struck a match and lit his cigar. The light showed a pale, square-jawed face with keen eyes, and a little white scar near his right eyebrow. His scarfpin was a large diamond, oddly set.

"Twenty years ago to-night," said the man, "I dined here at 'Big Joe' Brady's with Jimmy Wells, my best chum, and the finest chap in the world. He and I were raised here in New York, just like two brothers, together. I was eighteen and Jimmy was twenty. The next morning I was to start for the West to make my fortune. You couldn't have dragged Jimmy out of New York; he thought it was the only place on earth. Well, we agreed that night that we would meet here again exactly twenty years from that date and time, no matter what our conditions might be or from what distance we might have to come. We figured that in twenty years each of us ought to have our destiny worked out and our fortunes made, whatever they were going to be."

"It sounds pretty interesting," said the policeman. "Rather a long time between meets, though, it seems to me. Haven't you heard from your friend since you left?"

"Well, yes, for a time we corresponded," said the other. "But after a year or two we lost track of each other. You see, the West is a pretty big proposition, and I kept hustling around over it pretty lively. But I know Jimmy will meet me here if he's alive, for he always was the truest, stanchest old chap in the world. He'll never forget. I came a thousand miles to stand in this door to-night, and it's worth it if my old partner turns up."

The waiting man pulled out a handsome watch, the lids of it set with small diamonds.

"Three minutes to ten," he announced. "It was exactly ten o'clock when we parted here at the restaurant door."

"Did pretty well out West, didn't you?" asked the policeman.

"You bet! I hope Jimmy has done half as well. He was a kind of plodder, though, good fellow as he was. I've had to compete with some of the sharpest wits going to get my pile. A man gets in a groove in New York. It takes the West to put a razor-edge on him."

The policeman twirled his club and took a step or two.

"I'll be on my way. Hope your friend comes around all right. Going to call time on him sharp?"

"I should say not!" said the other. "I'll give him half an hour at least. If Jimmy is alive on earth he'll be here by that time. So long, officer."

"Good-night, sir," said the policeman, passing on along his beat, trying doors as he went.

There was now a fine, cold drizzle falling, and the wind had risen from its uncertain puffs into a steady blow. The few foot passengers astir in that quarter hurried dismally and silently along with coat collars turned high and pocketed hands. And in the door of the hardware store the man who had come a thousand miles to fill an appointment, uncertain almost to absurdity, with the friend of his youth, smoked his cigar and waited.

About twenty minutes he waited, and then a tall man in a long overcoat, with collar turned up to his ears, hurried across from the opposite side of the street. He went directly to the waiting man.

"Is that you, Bob?" he asked, doubtfully.

"Is that you, Jimmy Wells?" cried the man in the door.

"Bless my heart!" exclaimed the new arrival, grasping both the other's hands with his own. "It's Bob, sure as fate. I was certain I'd find you here if you were still in existence. Well, well, well!—twenty years is a long time. The old restaurant's gone, Bob; I wish it had lasted, so we could have had another dinner there. How has the West treated you, old man?"

"Bully; it has given me everything I asked it for. You've changed lots, Jimmy. I never thought you were so tall by two or three inches."

"Oh, I grew a bit after I was twenty."

"Doing well in New York, Jimmy?"

"Moderately. I have a position in one of the city departments. Come on, Bob; we'll go around to a place I know of, and have a good long talk about old times."

The two men started up the street, arm in arm. The man from the West, his egotism enlarged by success, was beginning to outline the history of his career. The other, submerged in his overcoat, listened with interest.

At the corner stood a drug store, brilliant with electric lights. When they came into this glare each of them turned simultaneously to gaze upon the other's face.

The man from the West stopped suddenly and released his arm.

"You're not Jimmy Wells," he snapped. "Twenty years is a long time, but not long enough to change a man's nose from a Roman to a pug."

"It sometimes changes a good man into a bad one," said the tall man. "You've been under arrest for ten minutes, 'Silky' Bob. Chicago thinks you may have dropped over our way and wires us she wants to have a chat with you. Going quietly, are you? That's sensible. Now, before we go on to the station here's a note I was asked to hand you. You may read it here at the window. It's from Patrolman Wells."

The man from the West unfolded the little piece of paper handed him. His hand was steady when he began to read, but it trembled a little by the time he had finished. The note was rather short.

> Bob: I was at the appointed place on time. When you struck the match to light your cigar I saw it was the face of the man wanted in Chicago. Somehow I couldn't do it myself, so I went around and got a plain clothes man to do the job.
>
> JIMMY.

A COSMOPOLITE IN A CAFÉ

At midnight the café was crowded. By some chance the little table at which I sat had escaped the eye of incomers, and two vacant chairs at it extended their arms with venal hospitality to the influx of patrons.

And then a cosmopolite sat in one of them, and I was glad, for I held a theory that since Adam no true citizen of the world has existed. We hear of them, and we see foreign labels on much luggage, but we find travellers instead of cosmopolites.

I invoke your consideration of the scene—the marble-topped tables, the range of leather-upholstered wall seats, the gay company, the ladies dressed in demi-state toilets, speaking in an exquisite visible chorus of taste, economy, opulence or art; the sedulous and largess-loving garçons, the music wisely catering to all with its raids upon the composers; the mélange of talk and laughter—and, if you will, the Würzburger in the tall glass cones that bend to your lips as a ripe cherry sways on its branch to the beak of a robber jay. I was told by a sculptor from Mauch Chunk that the scene was truly Parisian.

My cosmopolite was named E. Rushmore Coglan, and he will be heard from next summer at Coney Island. He is to establish a new "attraction" there, he informed me, offering kingly diversion. And then his conversation rang along parallels of latitude and longitude. He took the great, round world in his hand, so to speak, familiarly, contemptuously, and it seemed no larger than the seed of a Maraschino cherry in a table d'hôte grape fruit. He spoke disrespectfully of the equator, he skipped from continent to continent, he derided the zones, he mopped up the high seas with his napkin. With a wave of his hand he would speak of a certain bazaar in Hyderabad. Whiff! He would have you on skis in Lapland. Zip! Now you rode the breakers with the Kanakas at Kealaikahiki. Presto! He dragged you through an Arkansas post-oak swamp, let you dry for a moment on the alkali plains of his Idaho ranch, then whirled you into the society of Viennese archdukes. Anon he would be telling you of a cold he acquired in a Chicago lake breeze and how old Escamila cured it in Buenos Ayres with a hot infusion of the chuchula weed. You would have addressed a letter to "E. Rushmore Coglan, Esq., the Earth, Solar System, the Universe," and have mailed it, feeling confident that it would be delivered to him.

I was sure that I had found at last the one true cosmopolite since Adam, and I listened to his worldwide discourse fearful lest I should discover in it the local note of the mere globe-trotter. But his opinions never fluttered or drooped; he was as impartial to cities, countries and continents as the winds or gravitation.

And as E. Rushmore Coglan prattled of this little planet I thought with glee of a great almost-cosmopolite who wrote for the whole world and dedicated himself to Bombay. In a poem he has to say that there is pride and rivalry between the cities of the earth, and that "the men that breed from them, they traffic up and down, but cling to their cities' hem as a child to the mother's gown." And whenever they walk "by roaring streets unknown" they remember their native city "most faithful, foolish, fond; making her mere-breathed name their bond upon their bond." And my glee was roused because I had caught Mr. Kipling napping. Here I had found a man not made from dust; one who had no narrow boasts of birthplace or country, one who, if he bragged at all, would brag of his whole round globe against the Martians and the inhabitants of the Moon.

Expression on these subjects was precipitated from E. Rushmore Coglan by the third corner to our table. While Coglan was describing to me the topography along the Siberian Railway the orchestra glided into a medley. The concluding air was "Dixie," and as the exhilarating notes tumbled forth they were almost overpowered by a great clapping of hands from almost every table.

It is worth a paragraph to say that this remarkable scene can be witnessed every evening in numerous cafés in the City of New York. Tons of brew have been consumed over theories to account for it. Some have conjectured hastily that all Southerners in town hie themselves to cafés at nightfall. This applause of the "rebel" air in a Northern city does puzzle a little; but it is not insolvable. The war with Spain, many years' generous mint and watermelon crops, a few long-shot winners at the New Orleans race-track, and the brilliant banquets given by the Indiana and Kansas citizens who compose the North Carolina Society have made the South rather a "fad" in Manhattan. Your manicure will lisp softly that your left forefinger reminds her so much of a gentleman's in Richmond, Va. Oh, certainly; but many a lady has to work now—the war, you know.

When "Dixie" was being played a dark-haired young man sprang up from somewhere with a Mosby guerrilla yell and waved frantically his soft-brimmed hat. Then he strayed through the smoke, dropped into the vacant chair at our table and pulled out cigarettes.

The evening was at the period when reserve is thawed. One of us mentioned three Würzburgers to the waiter; the dark-haired young man acknowledged his inclusion in the order by a smile and a nod. I hastened to ask him a question because I wanted to try out a theory I had.

"Would you mind telling me," I began, "whether you are from—"

The fist of E. Rushmore Coglan banged the table and I was jarred into silence.

"Excuse me," said he, "but that's a question I never like to hear asked. What does it matter where a man is from? Is it fair to judge a man by his post-office address? Why, I've seen Kentuckians who hated whiskey, Virginians who weren't descended from Pocahontas, Indianians who hadn't written a novel, Mexicans who didn't wear velvet trousers with silver dollars sewed along the seams, funny Englishmen, spendthrift Yankees, cold-blooded Southerners, narrow-minded Westerners, and New Yorkers who were too busy to stop for an hour on the street to watch a one-armed grocer's clerk do up cranberries in paper bags. Let a man be a man and don't handicap him with the label of any section."

"Pardon me," I said, "but my curiosity was not altogether an idle one. I know the South, and when the band plays 'Dixie' I like to observe. I have formed the belief that the man who applauds that air with special violence and ostensible sectional loyalty is invariably a native of either Secaucus, N.J., or the district between Murray Hill Lyceum and the Harlem River, this city. I was about to put my opinion to the test by inquiring of this gentleman when you interrupted with your own—larger theory, I must confess."

And now the dark-haired young man spoke to me, and it became evident that his mind also moved along its own set of grooves.

"I should like to be a periwinkle," said he, mysteriously, "on the top of a valley, and sing tooralloo-ralloo."

This was clearly too obscure, so I turned again to Coglan.

"I've been around the world twelve times," said he. "I know an Esquimau in Upernavik who sends to Cincinnati for his neckties, and I saw a goat-herder in Uruguay who won a prize in a Battle Creek breakfast food puzzle competition. I pay rent on a room in Cairo, Egypt, and another in Yokohama all the year around. I've got slippers waiting for me in a tea-house in Shanghai, and I don't have to tell 'em how to cook my eggs in Rio de Janeiro or Seattle. It's a mighty little old world. What's the use of bragging about being from the North, or the South, or the old manor house in the dale, or Euclid avenue, Cleveland, or Pike's Peak, or Fairfax County, Va., or Hooligan's Flats or any place? It'll be a better world when we quit being fools about some mildewed town or ten acres of swampland just because we happened to be born there."

"You seem to be a genuine cosmopolite," I said admiringly. "But it also seems that you would decry patriotism."

"A relic of the stone age," declared Coglan, warmly. "We are all brothers—Chinamen, Englishmen, Zulus, Patagonians and the people in the bend of the Kaw River. Some day all this petty pride in one's city or State or section or country will be wiped out, and we'll all be citizens of the world, as we ought to be."

"But while you are wandering in foreign lands," I persisted, "do not your thoughts revert to some spot—some dear and—"

"Nary a spot," interrupted E. R. Coglan, flippantly. "The terrestrial, globular, planetary hunk of matter, slightly flattened at the poles, and known as the Earth, is my abode. I've met a good many object-bound citizens of this country abroad. I've seen men from Chicago sit in a gondola in Venice on a moonlight night and brag about their drainage canal. I've seen a Southerner on being introduced to the King of England hand that monarch, without batting his eyes, the information that his grand-aunt on his mother's side was related by marriage to the Perkinses, of Charleston. I knew a New Yorker who was kidnapped for ransom by some Afghanistan bandits. His people sent over the money and he came back to Kabul with the agent. 'Afghanistan?' the natives said to him through an interpreter. 'Well, not so slow, do you think?' 'Oh, I don't know,' says he, and he begins to tell them about a cab driver at Sixth avenue and Broadway. Those ideas don't suit me. I'm not tied down to anything that isn't 8,000 miles in diameter. Just put me down as E. Rushmore Coglan, citizen of the terrestrial sphere."

My cosmopolite made a large adieu and left me, for he thought he saw some one through the chatter and smoke whom he knew. So I was left with the would-be periwinkle, who was reduced to Würzburger without further ability to voice his aspirations to perch, melodious, upon the summit of a valley.

I sat reflecting upon my evident cosmopolite and wondering how the poet had managed to miss him. He was my discovery and I believed in him. How was it? "The men that breed from them they traffic up and down, but cling to their cities' hem as a child to the mother's gown."

Not so E. Rushmore Coglan. With the whole world for his—

My meditations were interrupted by a tremendous noise and conflict in another part of the café. I saw above the heads of the seated patrons E. Rushmore Coglan and a stranger to me engaged in terrific battle. They fought between the tables like Titans, and glasses crashed, and men caught their hats up and were knocked down, and a brunette screamed, and a blonde began to sing "Teasing."

My cosmopolite was sustaining the pride and reputation of the Earth when the waiters closed in on both combatants with their famous flying wedge formation and bore them outside, still resisting.

I called McCarthy, one of the French garçons, and asked him the cause of the conflict.

"The man with the red tie" (that was my cosmopolite), said he, "got hot on account of things said about the bum sidewalks and water supply of the place he come from by the other guy."

"Why," said I, bewildered, "that man is a citizen of the world—a cosmopolite. He—"

"Originally from Mattawamkeag, Maine, he said," continued McCarthy, "and he wouldn't stand for no knockin' the place."

THE COMING-OUT OF MAGGIE

Every Saturday night the Clover Leaf Social Club gave a hop in the hall of the Give and Take Athletic Association on the East Side. In order to attend one of these dances you must be a member of the Give and Take—or, if you belong to the division that starts off with the right foot in waltzing, you must work in Rhinegold's paper-box factory. Still, any Clover Leaf was privileged to escort or be escorted by an outsider to a single dance. But mostly each Give and Take brought the paper-box girl that he affected; and few strangers could boast of having shaken a foot at the regular hops.

Maggie Toole, on account of her dull eyes, broad mouth and left-handed style of footwork in the two-step, went to the dances with Anna McCarty and her "fellow." Anna and Maggie worked side by side in the factory, and were the greatest chums ever. So Anna always made Jimmy Burns take her by Maggie's house every Saturday night so that her friend could go to the dance with them.

The Give and Take Athletic Association lived up to its name. The hall of the association in Orchard street was fitted out with muscle-making inventions. With the fibres thus builded up the members were wont to engage the police and rival social and athletic organisations in joyous combat. Between these more serious occupations the Saturday night hop with the paper-box factory girls came as a refining influence and as an efficient screen. For sometimes the tip went 'round, and if you were among the elect that tiptoed up the dark back stairway you might see as neat and satisfying a little welter-weight affair to a finish as ever happened inside the ropes.

On Saturdays Rhinegold's paper-box factory closed at 3 P. M. On one such afternoon Anna and Maggie walked homeward together. At Maggie's door Anna said, as usual: "Be ready at seven, sharp, Mag; and Jimmy and me'll come by for you."

But what was this? Instead of the customary humble and grateful thanks from the non-escorted one there was to be perceived a high-poised head, a prideful dimpling at the corners of a broad mouth, and almost a sparkle in a dull brown eye.

"Thanks, Anna," said Maggie; "but you and Jimmy needn't bother to-night. I've a gentleman friend that's coming 'round to escort me to the hop."

The comely Anna pounced upon her friend, shook her, chided and beseeched her. Maggie Toole catch a fellow! Plain, dear, loyal, unattractive Maggie, so sweet as a chum, so unsought for a two-step or a moonlit bench in the little park. How was it? When did it happen? Who was it?

"You'll see to-night," said Maggie, flushed with the wine of the first grapes she had gathered in Cupid's vineyard. "He's swell all right. He's two inches taller than Jimmy, and an up-to-date dresser. I'll introduce him, Anna, just as soon as we get to the hall."

Anna and Jimmy were among the first Clover Leafs to arrive that evening. Anna's eyes were brightly fixed upon the door of the hall to catch the first glimpse of her friend's "catch."

At 8:30 Miss Toole swept into the hall with her escort. Quickly her triumphant eye discovered her chum under the wing of her faithful Jimmy.

"Oh, gee!" cried Anna, "Mag ain't made a hit—oh, no! Swell fellow? well, I guess! Style? Look at 'um."

"Go as far as you like," said Jimmy, with sandpaper in his voice. "Cop him out if you want him. These new guys always win out with the push. Don't mind me. He don't squeeze all the limes, I guess. Huh!"

"Shut up, Jimmy. You know what I mean. I'm glad for Mag. First fellow she ever had. Oh, here they come."

Across the floor Maggie sailed like a coquettish yacht convoyed by a stately cruiser. And truly, her companion justified the encomiums of the faithful chum. He stood two inches taller than the average Give and Take athlete; his dark hair curled; his eyes and his teeth flashed whenever he bestowed his frequent smiles. The young men of the Clover Leaf Club pinned not their faith to the graces of person as much as they did to its prowess, its achievements in hand-to-hand conflicts, and its preservation from the legal duress that constantly menaced it. The member of the association who would bind a paper-box maiden to his conquering chariot scorned to employ Beau Brummel airs. They were not considered honourable methods of warfare. The swelling biceps, the coat straining at its buttons over the chest, the air of conscious conviction of the supereminence of the male in the cosmogony of creation, even a calm display of bow legs as subduing and enchanting agents in the gentle tourneys of Cupid—these were the approved arms and ammunition of the Clover Leaf gallants. They viewed, then, genuflexions and alluring poses of this visitor with their chins at a new angle.

"A friend of mine, Mr. Terry O'Sullivan," was Maggie's formula of introduction. She led him around the room, presenting him to each new-arriving Clover Leaf. Almost was she pretty now, with the unique luminosity in her eyes that comes to a girl with her first suitor and a kitten with its first mouse.

"Maggie Toole's got a fellow at last," was the word that went round among the paper-box girls. "Pipe Mag's floor-walker"—thus the Give and Takes expressed their indifferent contempt.

Usually at the weekly hops Maggie kept a spot on the wall warm with her back. She felt and showed so much gratitude whenever a self-sacrificing partner invited her to dance that his pleasure was cheapened and diminished. She had even grown used to noticing Anna joggle the reluctant Jimmy with her elbow as a signal for him to invite her chum to walk over his feet through a two-step.

But to-night the pumpkin had turned to a coach and six. Terry O'Sullivan was a victorious Prince Charming, and Maggie Toole winged her first butterfly flight. And though our tropes of fairyland be mixed with those of entomology they shall not spill one drop of ambrosia from the rose-crowned melody of Maggie's one perfect night.

The girls besieged her for introductions to her "fellow." The Clover Leaf young men, after two years of blindness, suddenly perceived charms in Miss Toole. They flexed their compelling muscles before her and bespoke her for the dance.

Thus she scored; but to Terry O'Sullivan the honours of the evening fell thick and fast. He shook his curls; he smiled and went easily through the seven motions for acquiring grace in your own room before an open window ten minutes each day. He danced like a faun; he introduced manner and style and atmosphere; his words came trippingly upon his tongue, and—he waltzed twice in succession with the paper-box girl that Dempsey Donovan brought.

Dempsey was the leader of the association. He wore a dress suit, and could chin the bar twice with one hand. He was one of "Big Mike" O'Sullivan's lieutenants, and was never troubled by trouble. No cop dared to arrest him. Whenever he broke a pushcart man's head or shot a member of the Heinrick B. Sweeney Outing and Literary Association in the kneecap, an officer would drop around and say:

"The Cap'n 'd like to see ye a few minutes round to the office whin ye have time, Dempsey, me boy."

But there would be sundry gentlemen there with large gold fob chains and black cigars; and somebody would tell a funny story, and then Dempsey would go back and work half an hour with the six-pound dumbbells. So, doing a tight-rope act on a wire stretched across Niagara was a safe terpsichorean performance compared with waltzing twice with Dempsey Donovan's paper-box girl. At 10 o'clock the jolly round face of "Big Mike" O'Sullivan shone at the door for five minutes upon the scene. He always looked in for five minutes, smiled at the girls and handed out real perfectos to the delighted boys.

Dempsey Donovan was at his elbow instantly, talking rapidly. "Big Mike" looked carefully at the dancers, smiled, shook his head and departed.

The music stopped. The dancers scattered to the chairs along the walls. Terry O'Sullivan, with his entrancing bow, relinquished a pretty girl in blue to her partner and started back to find Maggie. Dempsey intercepted him in the middle of the floor.

Some fine instinct that Rome must have bequeathed to us caused nearly every one to turn and look at them—there was a subtle feeling that two gladiators had met in the arena. Two or three Give and Takes with tight coat sleeves drew nearer.

"One moment, Mr. O'Sullivan," said Dempsey. "I hope you're enjoying yourself. Where did you say you live?"

The two gladiators were well matched. Dempsey had, perhaps, ten pounds of weight to give away. The O'Sullivan had breadth with quickness. Dempsey had a glacial eye, a dominating slit of a mouth, an indestructible jaw, a complexion like a belle's and the coolness of a champion. The visitor showed more fire in his contempt and less control over his conspicuous sneer. They were enemies by the law written when the rocks were molten. They were each too splendid, too mighty, too incomparable to divide pre-eminence. One only must survive.

"I live on Grand," said O'Sullivan, insolently; "and no trouble to find me at home. Where do you live?"

Dempsey ignored the question.

"You say your name's O'Sullivan," he went on. "Well, 'Big Mike' says he never saw you before."

"Lots of things he never saw," said the favourite of the hop.

"As a rule," went on Dempsey, huskily sweet, "O'Sullivans in this district know one another. You escorted one of our lady members here, and we want a chance to make good. If you've got a family tree let's see a few historical O'Sullivan buds come out on it. Or do you want us to dig it out of you by the roots?"

"Suppose you mind your own business," suggested O'Sullivan, blandly.

Dempsey's eye brightened. He held up an inspired forefinger as though a brilliant idea had struck him.

"I've got it now," he said cordially. "It was just a little mistake. You ain't no O'Sullivan. You are a ring-tailed monkey. Excuse us for not recognising you at first."

O'Sullivan's eye flashed. He made a quick movement, but Andy Geoghan was ready and caught his arm.

Dempsey nodded at Andy and William McMahan, the secretary of the club, and walked rapidly toward a door at the rear of the hall. Two other members of the Give and Take Association swiftly joined the little group. Terry O'Sullivan was now in the hands of the Board of

Rules and Social Referees. They spoke to him briefly and softly, and conducted him out through the same door at the rear.

This movement on the part of the Clover Leaf members requires a word of elucidation. Back of the association hall was a smaller room rented by the club. In this room personal difficulties that arose on the ballroom floor were settled, man to man, with the weapons of nature, under the supervision of the board. No lady could say that she had witnessed a fight at a Clover Leaf hop in several years. Its gentlemen members guaranteed that.

So easily and smoothly had Dempsey and the board done their preliminary work that many in the hall had not noticed the checking of the fascinating O'Sullivan's social triumph. Among these was Maggie. She looked about for her escort.

"Smoke up!" said Rose Cassidy. "Wasn't you on? Demps Donovan picked a scrap with your Lizzie-boy, and they've waltzed out to the slaughter room with him. How's my hair look done up this way, Mag?"

Maggie laid a hand on the bosom of her cheesecloth waist.

"Gone to fight with Dempsey!" she said, breathlessly. "They've got to be stopped. Dempsey Donovan can't fight him. Why, he'll—he'll kill him!"

"Ah, what do you care?" said Rosa. "Don't some of 'em fight every hop?"

But Maggie was off, darting her zig-zag way through the maze of dancers. She burst through the rear door into the dark hall and then threw her solid shoulder against the door of the room of single combat. It gave way, and in the instant that she entered her eye caught the scene—the Board standing about with open watches; Dempsey

Donovan in his shirt sleeves dancing, light-footed, with the wary grace of the modern pugilist, within easy reach of his adversary; Terry O'Sullivan standing with arms folded and a murderous look in his dark eyes. And without slacking the speed of her entrance she leaped forward with a scream—leaped in time to catch and hang upon the arm of O'Sullivan that was suddenly uplifted, and to whisk from it the long, bright stiletto that he had drawn from his bosom.

The knife fell and rang upon the floor. Cold steel drawn in the rooms of the Give and Take Association! Such a thing had never happened before. Every one stood motionless for a minute. Andy Geoghan kicked the stiletto with the toe of his shoe curiously, like an antiquarian who has come upon some ancient weapon unknown to his learning.

And then O'Sullivan hissed something unintelligible between his teeth. Dempsey and the board exchanged looks. And then Dempsey looked at O'Sullivan without anger, as one looks at a stray dog, and nodded his head in the direction of the door.

"The back stairs, Giuseppi," he said, briefly. "Somebody'll pitch your hat down after you."

Maggie walked up to Dempsey Donovan. There was a brilliant spot of red in her cheeks, down which slow tears were running. But she looked him bravely in the eye.

"I knew it, Dempsey," she said, as her eyes grew dull even in their tears. "I knew he was a Guinea. His name's Tony Spinelli. I hurried in when they told me you and him was scrappin'. Them Guineas always carries knives. But you don't understand, Dempsey. I never had a fellow in my life. I got tired of comin' with Anna and Jimmy every night, so I fixed it with him to call himself O'Sullivan, and brought him along. I knew there'd be nothin' doin' for him if he came as a Dago. I guess I'll resign from the club now."

Dempsey turned to Andy Geoghan.

"Chuck that cheese slicer out of the window," he said, "and tell 'em inside that Mr. O'Sullivan has had a telephone message to go down to Tammany Hall."

And then he turned back to Maggie.

"Say, Mag," he said, "I'll see you home. And how about next Saturday night? Will you come to the hop with me if I call around for you?"

It was remarkable how quickly Maggie's eyes could change from dull to a shining brown.

"With you, Dempsey?" she stammered. "Say—will a duck swim?"

THE ROMANCE OF A BUSY BROKER

Pitcher, confidential clerk in the office of Harvey Maxwell, broker, allowed a look of mild interest and surprise to visit his usually expressionless countenance when his employer briskly entered at half past nine in company with his young lady stenographer. With a snappy "Good-morning, Pitcher," Maxwell dashed at his desk as though he were intending to leap over it, and then plunged into the great heap of letters and telegrams waiting there for him.

The young lady had been Maxwell's stenographer for a year. She was beautiful in a way that was decidedly unstenographic. She forewent the pomp of the alluring pompadour. She wore no chains, bracelets or lockets. She had not the air of being about to accept an invitation to luncheon. Her dress was grey and plain, but it fitted her figure with fidelity and discretion. In her neat black turban hat was the gold-green wing of a macaw. On this morning she was softly and shyly radiant. Her eyes were dreamily bright, her cheeks genuine peachblow, her expression a happy one, tinged with reminiscence.

Pitcher, still mildly curious, noticed a difference in her ways this morning. Instead of going straight into the adjoining room, where her desk was, she lingered, slightly irresolute, in the outer office. Once she moved over by Maxwell's desk, near enough for him to be aware of her presence.

The machine sitting at that desk was no longer a man; it was a busy New York broker, moved by buzzing wheels and uncoiling springs.

"Well—what is it? Anything?" asked Maxwell sharply. His opened mail lay like a bank of stage snow on his crowded desk. His keen grey eye, impersonal and brusque, flashed upon her half impatiently.

"Nothing," answered the stenographer, moving away with a little smile.

"Mr. Pitcher," she said to the confidential clerk, "did Mr. Maxwell say anything yesterday about engaging another stenographer?"

"He did," answered Pitcher. "He told me to get another one. I notified the agency yesterday afternoon to send over a few samples this morning. It's 9.45 o'clock, and not a single picture hat or piece of pineapple chewing gum has showed up yet."

"I will do the work as usual, then," said the young lady, "until some one comes to fill the place." And she went to her desk at once and hung the black turban hat with the gold-green macaw wing in its accustomed place.

He who has been denied the spectacle of a busy Manhattan broker during a rush of business is handicapped for the profession of anthropology. The poet sings of the "crowded hour of glorious life." The broker's hour is not only crowded, but the minutes and seconds are hanging to all the straps and packing both front and rear platforms.

And this day was Harvey Maxwell's busy day. The ticker began to reel out jerkily its fitful coils of tape, the desk telephone had a chronic attack of buzzing. Men began to throng into the office and call at him over the railing, jovially, sharply, viciously, excitedly. Messenger boys ran in and out with messages and telegrams. The clerks in the office jumped about like sailors during a storm. Even Pitcher's face relaxed into something resembling animation.

On the Exchange there were hurricanes and landslides and snowstorms and glaciers and volcanoes, and those elemental disturbances were reproduced in miniature in the broker's offices. Maxwell shoved his chair against the wall and transacted business after the manner of a toe dancer. He jumped from ticker to 'phone, from desk to door with the trained agility of a harlequin.

In the midst of this growing and important stress the broker became suddenly aware of a high-rolled fringe of golden hair under a nodding canopy of velvet and ostrich tips, an imitation sealskin sacque and a string of beads as large as hickory nuts, ending near the floor with a silver heart. There was a self-possessed young lady connected with these accessories; and Pitcher was there to construe her.

"Lady from the Stenographer's Agency to see about the position," said Pitcher.

Maxwell turned half around, with his hands full of papers and ticker tape.

"What position?" he asked, with a frown.

"Position of stenographer," said Pitcher. "You told me yesterday to call them up and have one sent over this morning."

"You are losing your mind, Pitcher," said Maxwell. "Why should I have given you any such instructions? Miss Leslie has given perfect satisfaction during the year she has been here. The place is hers as long as she chooses to retain it. There's no place open here, madam. Countermand that order with the agency, Pitcher, and don't bring any more of 'em in here."

The silver heart left the office, swinging and banging itself independently against the office furniture as it indignantly departed. Pitcher seized a moment to remark to the bookkeeper that the "old man" seemed to get more absent-minded and forgetful every day of the world.

The rush and pace of business grew fiercer and faster. On the floor they were pounding half a dozen stocks in which Maxwell's customers were heavy investors. Orders to buy and sell were coming and going as swift as the flight of swallows. Some of his own holdings were imperilled, and the man was working like some high-geared, delicate, strong machine—strung to full tension, going at full speed, accurate, never hesitating, with the proper word and decision and act ready and prompt as clockwork. Stocks and bonds, loans and mortgages, margins and securities—here was a world of finance, and there was no room in it for the human world or the world of nature.

When the luncheon hour drew near there came a slight lull in the uproar.

Maxwell stood by his desk with his hands full of telegrams and memoranda, with a fountain pen over his right ear and his hair hanging in disorderly strings over his forehead. His window was open, for the beloved janitress Spring had turned on a little warmth through the waking registers of the earth.

And through the window came a wandering—perhaps a lost—odour—a delicate, sweet odour of lilac that fixed the broker for a moment immovable. For this odour belonged to Miss Leslie; it was her own, and hers only.

The odour brought her vividly, almost tangibly before him. The world of finance dwindled suddenly to a speck. And she was in the next room—twenty steps away.

"By George, I'll do it now," said Maxwell, half aloud. "I'll ask her now. I wonder I didn't do it long ago."

He dashed into the inner office with the haste of a short trying to cover. He charged upon the desk of the stenographer.

She looked up at him with a smile. A soft pink crept over her cheek, and her eyes were kind and frank. Maxwell leaned one elbow on her desk. He still clutched fluttering papers with both hands and the pen was above his ear.

"Miss Leslie," he began hurriedly, "I have but a moment to spare. I want to say something in that moment. Will you be my wife? I haven't had time to make love to you in the ordinary way, but I really do love you. Talk quick, please—those fellows are clubbing the stuffing out of Union Pacific."

"Oh, what are you talking about?" exclaimed the young lady. She rose to her feet and gazed upon him, round-eyed.

"Don't you understand?" said Maxwell, restively. "I want you to marry me. I love you, Miss Leslie. I wanted to tell you, and I snatched a minute when things had slackened up a bit. They're calling me for the 'phone now. Tell 'em to wait a minute, Pitcher. Won't you, Miss Leslie?"

The stenographer acted very queerly. At first she seemed overcome with amazement; then tears flowed from her wondering eyes; and then she smiled sunnily through them, and one of her arms slid tenderly about the broker's neck.

"I know now," she said, softly. "It's this old business that has driven everything else out of your head for the time. I was frightened at first. Don't you remember, Harvey? We were married last evening at 8 o'clock in the Little Church Around the Corner."

A SERVICE OF LOVE

When one loves one's Art no service seems too hard.

That is our premise. This story shall draw a conclusion from it, and show at the same time that the premise is incorrect. That will be a new thing in logic, and a feat in story-telling somewhat older than the great wall of China.

Joe Larrabee came out of the post-oak flats of the Middle West pulsing with a genius for pictorial art. At six he drew a picture of the town pump with a prominent citizen passing it hastily. This effort was framed and hung in the drug store window by the side of the ear of corn with an uneven number of rows. At twenty he left for New York with a flowing necktie and a capital tied up somewhat closer.

Delia Caruthers did things in six octaves so promisingly in a pine-tree village in the South that her relatives chipped in enough in her chip hat for her to go "North" and "finish." They could not see her f—, but that is our story.

Joe and Delia met in an atelier where a number of art and music students had gathered to discuss chiaroscuro, Wagner, music, Rembrandt's works, pictures, Waldteufel, wall paper, Chopin and Oolong.

Joe and Delia became enamoured one of the other, or each of the other, as you please, and in a short time were married—for (see above), when one loves one's Art no service seems too hard.

Mr. and Mrs. Larrabee began housekeeping in a flat. It was a lonesome flat—something like the A sharp way down at the left-hand end of the keyboard. And they were happy; for they had their Art, and they had each other. And my advice to the rich young man would be—sell all thou hast, and give it to the poor—janitor for the privilege of living in a flat with your Art and your Delia.

Flat-dwellers shall indorse my dictum that theirs is the only true happiness. If a home is happy it cannot fit too close—let the dresser collapse and become a billiard table; let the mantel turn to a rowing machine, the escritoire to a spare bedchamber, the washstand to an upright piano; let the four walls come together, if they will, so you and your Delia are between. But if home be the other kind, let it be wide and long—enter you at the Golden Gate, hang your hat on Hatteras, your cape on Cape Horn and go out by the Labrador.

Joe was painting in the class of the great Magister—you know his fame. His fees are high; his lessons are light—his high-lights have brought him renown. Delia was studying under Rosenstock—you know his repute as a disturber of the piano keys.

They were mighty happy as long as their money lasted. So is every—but I will not be cynical. Their aims were very clear and defined. Joe was to become capable very soon of turning out pictures that old gentlemen with thin side-whiskers and thick pocketbooks would sandbag one another in his studio for the privilege of buying. Delia was to become familiar and then contemptuous with Music, so that when she saw the orchestra seats and boxes unsold she could have sore throat and lobster in a private dining-room and refuse to go on the stage.

But the best, in my opinion, was the home life in the little flat—the ardent, voluble chats after the day's study; the cozy dinners and fresh, light breakfasts; the interchange of ambitions—ambitions interwoven each with the other's or else inconsiderable—the mutual help and inspiration; and—overlook my artlessness—stuffed olives and cheese sandwiches at 11 p.m.

But after a while Art flagged. It sometimes does, even if some switchman doesn't flag it. Everything going out and nothing coming in, as the vulgarians say. Money was lacking to pay Mr. Magister and Herr Rosenstock their prices. When one loves one's Art no service seems too hard. So, Delia said she must give music lessons to keep the chafing dish bubbling.

For two or three days she went out canvassing for pupils. One evening she came home elated.

"Joe, dear," she said, gleefully, "I've a pupil. And, oh, the loveliest people! General—General A. B. Pinkney's daughter—on Seventy-first street. Such a splendid house, Joe—you ought to see the front door! Byzantine I think you would call it. And inside! Oh, Joe, I never saw anything like it before.

"My pupil is his daughter Clementina. I dearly love her already. She's a delicate thing—dresses always in white; and the sweetest, simplest manners! Only eighteen years old. I'm to give three lessons a week; and, just think, Joe! $5 a lesson. I don't mind it a bit; for when I get two or three more pupils I can resume my lessons with Herr Rosenstock. Now, smooth out that wrinkle between your brows, dear, and let's have a nice supper."

"That's all right for you, Dele," said Joe, attacking a can of peas with a carving knife and a hatchet, "but how about me? Do you think I'm going to let you hustle for wages while I philander in the regions of high art? Not by the bones of Benvenuto Cellini! I guess I can sell papers or lay cobblestones, and bring in a dollar or two."

Delia came and hung about his neck.

"Joe, dear, you are silly. You must keep on at your studies. It is not as if I had quit my music and gone to work at something else. While I teach I learn. I am always with my music. And we can live as happily as millionaires on $15 a week. You mustn't think of leaving Mr. Magister."

"All right," said Joe, reaching for the blue scalloped vegetable dish. "But I hate for you to be giving lessons. It isn't Art. But you're a trump and a dear to do it."

"When one loves one's Art no service seems too hard," said Delia.

"Magister praised the sky in that sketch I made in the park," said Joe. "And Tinkle gave me permission to hang two of them in his window. I may sell one if the right kind of a moneyed idiot sees them."

"I'm sure you will," said Delia, sweetly. "And now let's be thankful for Gen. Pinkney and this veal roast."

During all of the next week the Larrabees had an early breakfast. Joe was enthusiastic about some morning-effect sketches he was doing in Central Park, and Delia packed him off breakfasted, coddled, praised and kissed at 7 o'clock. Art is an engaging mistress. It was most times 7 o'clock when he returned in the evening.

At the end of the week Delia, sweetly proud but languid, triumphantly tossed three five-dollar bills on the 8×10 (inches) centre table of the 8×10 (feet) flat parlour.

"Sometimes," she said, a little wearily, "Clementina tries me. I'm afraid she doesn't practise enough, and I have to tell her the same things so often. And then she always dresses entirely in white, and that does get monotonous. But Gen. Pinkney is the dearest old man! I wish you could know him, Joe. He comes in sometimes when I am with Clementina at the piano—he is a widower, you know—and stands there pulling his white goatee. 'And how are the semiquavers and the demisemiquavers progressing?' he always asks.

"I wish you could see the wainscoting in that drawing-room, Joe! And those Astrakhan rug portières. And Clementina has such a funny little cough. I hope she is stronger than she looks. Oh, I really am getting attached to her, she is so gentle and high bred. Gen. Pinkney's brother was once Minister to Bolivia."

And then Joe, with the air of a Monte Cristo, drew forth a ten, a five, a two and a one—all legal tender notes—and laid them beside Delia's earnings.

"Sold that watercolour of the obelisk to a man from Peoria," he announced overwhelmingly.

"Don't joke with me," said Delia, "not from Peoria!"

"All the way. I wish you could see him, Dele. Fat man with a woollen muffler and a quill toothpick. He saw the sketch in Tinkle's window and thought it was a windmill at first. He was game, though, and bought it anyhow. He ordered another—an oil sketch of the Lackawanna freight depot—to take back with him. Music lessons! Oh, I guess Art is still in it."

"I'm so glad you've kept on," said Delia, heartily. "You're bound to win, dear. Thirty-three dollars! We never had so much to spend before. We'll have oysters to-night."

"And filet mignon with champignons," said Joe. "Where is the olive fork?"

On the next Saturday evening Joe reached home first. He spread his $18 on the parlour table and washed what seemed to be a great deal of dark paint from his hands.

Half an hour later Delia arrived, her right hand tied up in a shapeless bundle of wraps and bandages.

"How is this?" asked Joe after the usual greetings. Delia laughed, but not very joyously.

"Clementina," she explained, "insisted upon a Welsh rabbit after her lesson. She is such a queer girl. Welsh rabbits at 5 in the afternoon. The General was there. You should have seen him run for the chafing dish, Joe, just as if there wasn't a servant in the house. I know Clementina isn't in good health; she is so nervous. In serving the rabbit she spilled a great lot of it, boiling hot, over my hand and wrist.

150

It hurt awfully, Joe. And the dear girl was so sorry! But Gen. Pinkney!—Joe, that old man nearly went distracted. He rushed downstairs and sent somebody—they said the furnace man or somebody in the basement—out to a drug store for some oil and things to bind it up with. It doesn't hurt so much now."

"What's this?" asked Joe, taking the hand tenderly and pulling at some white strands beneath the bandages.

"It's something soft," said Delia, "that had oil on it. Oh, Joe, did you sell another sketch?" She had seen the money on the table.

"Did I?" said Joe; "just ask the man from Peoria. He got his depot to-day, and he isn't sure but he thinks he wants another parkscape and a view on the Hudson. What time this afternoon did you burn your hand, Dele?"

"Five o'clock, I think," said Dele, plaintively. "The iron—I mean the rabbit came off the fire about that time. You ought to have seen Gen. Pinkney, Joe, when—"

"Sit down here a moment, Dele," said Joe. He drew her to the couch, sat beside her and put his arm across her shoulders.

"What have you been doing for the last two weeks, Dele?" he asked.

She braved it for a moment or two with an eye full of love and stubbornness, and murmured a phrase or two vaguely of Gen. Pinkney; but at length down went her head and out came the truth and tears.

"I couldn't get any pupils," she confessed. "And I couldn't bear to have you give up your lessons; and I got a place ironing shirts in that big

Twenty-fourth street laundry. And I think I did very well to make up both General Pinkney and Clementina, don't you, Joe? And when a girl in the laundry set down a hot iron on my hand this afternoon I was all the way home making up that story about the Welsh rabbit. You're not angry, are you, Joe? And if I hadn't got the work you mightn't have sold your sketches to that man from Peoria."

"He wasn't from Peoria," said Joe, slowly.

"Well, it doesn't matter where he was from. How clever you are, Joe—and—kiss me, Joe—and what made you ever suspect that I wasn't giving music lessons to Clementina?"

"I didn't," said Joe, "until to-night. And I wouldn't have then, only I sent up this cotton waste and oil from the engine-room this afternoon for a girl upstairs who had her hand burned with a smoothing-iron. I've been firing the engine in that laundry for the last two weeks."

"And then you didn't—"

"My purchaser from Peoria," said Joe, "and Gen. Pinkney are both creations of the same art—but you wouldn't call it either painting or music."

And then they both laughed, and Joe began:

"When one loves one's Art no service seems—"

But Delia stopped him with her hand on his lips. "No," she said—"just 'When one loves.'"

MAN ABOUT TOWN

There were two or three things that I wanted to know. I do not care about a mystery. So I began to inquire.

It took me two weeks to find out what women carry in dress suit cases. And then I began to ask why a mattress is made in two pieces. This serious query was at first received with suspicion because it sounded like a conundrum. I was at last assured that its double form of construction was designed to make lighter the burden of woman, who makes up beds. I was so foolish as to persist, begging to know why, then, they were not made in two equal pieces; whereupon I was shunned.

The third draught that I craved from the fount of knowledge was enlightenment concerning the character known as A Man About Town. He was more vague in my mind than a type should be. We must have a concrete idea of anything, even if it be an imaginary idea, before we can comprehend it. Now, I have a mental picture of John Doe that is as clear as a steel engraving. His eyes are weak blue; he wears a brown vest and a shiny black serge coat. He stands always in the sunshine chewing something; and he keeps half-shutting his pocket knife and opening it again with his thumb. And, if the Man Higher Up is ever found, take my assurance for it, he will be a large, pale man with blue wristlets showing under his cuffs, and he will be sitting to have his shoes polished within sound of a bowling alley, and there will be somewhere about him turquoises.

But the canvas of my imagination, when it came to limning the Man About Town, was blank. I fancied that he had a detachable sneer (like the smile of the Cheshire cat) and attached cuffs; and that was all. Whereupon I asked a newspaper reporter about him.

"Why," said he, "a 'Man About Town' something between a 'rounder' and a 'clubman.' He isn't exactly—well, he fits in between Mrs. Fish's receptions and private boxing bouts. He doesn't—well, he doesn't belong either to the Lotos Club or to the Jerry McGeogheghan Galvanised Iron Workers' Apprentices' Left Hook Chowder Association. I don't exactly know how to describe him to you. You'll see him everywhere there's anything doing. Yes, I suppose he's a type. Dress clothes every evening; knows the ropes; calls every policeman and waiter in town by their first names. No; he never travels with the hydrogen derivatives. You generally see him alone or with another man."

My friend the reporter left me, and I wandered further afield. By this time the 3126 electric lights on the Rialto were alight. People passed, but they held me not. Paphian eyes rayed upon me, and left me unscathed. Diners, heimgangers, shop-girls, confidence men, panhandlers, actors, highwaymen, millionaires and outlanders hurried, skipped, strolled, sneaked, swaggered and scurried by me; but I took no note of them. I knew them all; I had read their hearts; they had served. I wanted my Man About Town. He was a type, and to drop him would be an error—a typograph—but no! let us continue.

Let us continue with a moral digression. To see a family reading the Sunday paper gratifies. The sections have been separated. Papa is earnestly scanning the page that pictures the young lady exercising before an open window, and bending—but there, there! Mamma is interested in trying to guess the missing letters in the word N_w Yo_k. The oldest girls are eagerly perusing the financial reports, for a certain young man remarked last Sunday night that he had taken a flyer in Q., X. & Z. Willie, the eighteen-year-old son, who attends the New York public school, is absorbed in the weekly article describing how to make over an old skirt, for he hopes to take a prize in sewing on graduation day.

Grandma is holding to the comic supplement with a two-hours' grip; and little Tottie, the baby, is rocking along the best she can with the real estate transfers. This view is intended to be reassuring, for it is desirable that a few lines of this story be skipped. For it introduces strong drink.

I went into a café to—and while it was being mixed I asked the man who grabs up your hot Scotch spoon as soon as you lay it down what he understood by the term, epithet, description, designation, characterisation or appellation, viz.: a "Man About Town."

"Why," said he, carefully, "it means a fly guy that's wise to the all-night push—see? It's a hot sport that you can't bump to the rail anywhere between the Flatirons—see? I guess that's about what it means."

I thanked him and departed.

On the sidewalk a Salvation lassie shook her contribution receptacle gently against my waistcoat pocket.

"Would you mind telling me," I asked her, "if you ever meet with the character commonly denominated as 'A Man About Town' during your daily wanderings?"

"I think I know whom you mean," she answered, with a gentle smile. "We see them in the same places night after night. They are the devil's body guard, and if the soldiers of any army are as faithful as they are, their commanders are well served. We go among them, diverting a few pennies from their wickedness to the Lord's service."

She shook the box again and I dropped a dime into it.

In front of a glittering hotel a friend of mine, a critic, was climbing from a cab. He seemed at leisure; and I put my question to him. He answered me conscientiously, as I was sure he would.

"There is a type of 'Man About Town' in New York," he answered. "The term is quite familiar to me, but I don't think I was ever called upon to define the character before. It would be difficult to point you out an exact specimen. I would say, offhand, that it is a man who had a hopeless case of the peculiar New York disease of wanting to see and know. At 6 o'clock each day life begins with him. He follows rigidly the conventions of dress and manners; but in the business of poking his nose into places where he does not belong he could give pointers to a civet cat or a jackdaw. He is the man who has chased Bohemia about the town from rathskeller to roof garden and from Hester street to Harlem until you can't find a place in the city where they don't cut their spaghetti with a knife. Your 'Man About Town' has done that. He is always on the scent of something new. He is curiosity, impudence and omnipresence. Hansoms were made for him, and gold-banded cigars; and the curse of music at dinner. There are not so many of him; but his minority report is adopted everywhere.

"I'm glad you brought up the subject; I've felt the influence of this nocturnal blight upon our city, but I never thought to analyse it before. I can see now that your 'Man About Town' should have been classified long ago. In his wake spring up wine agents and cloak models; and the orchestra plays 'Let's All Go Up to Maud's' for him, by request, instead of Händel. He makes his rounds every evening; while you and I see the elephant once a week. When the cigar store is raided, he winks at the officer, familiar with his ground, and walks away immune, while you and I search among the Presidents for names, and among the stars for addresses to give the desk sergeant."

My friend, the critic, paused to acquire breath for fresh eloquence. I seized my advantage.

"You have classified him," I cried with joy. "You have painted his portrait in the gallery of city types. But I must meet one face to face. I must study the Man About Town at first hand. Where shall I find him? How shall I know him?"

Without seeming to hear me, the critic went on. And his cab-driver was waiting for his fare, too.

"He is the sublimated essence of Butt-in; the refined, intrinsic extract of Rubber; the concentrated, purified, irrefutable, unavoidable spirit of Curiosity and Inquisitiveness. A new sensation is the breath in his nostrils; when his experience is exhausted he explores new fields with the indefatigability of a—"

"Excuse me," I interrupted, "but can you produce one of this type? It is a new thing to me. I must study it. I will search the town over until I find one. Its habitat must be here on Broadway."

"I am about to dine here," said my friend. "Come inside, and if there is a Man About Town present I will point him out to you. I know most of the regular patrons here."

"I am not dining yet," I said to him. "You will excuse me. I am going to find my Man About Town this night if I have to rake New York from the Battery to Little Coney Island."

I left the hotel and walked down Broadway. The pursuit of my type gave a pleasant savour of life and interest to the air I breathed. I was glad to be in a city so great, so complex and diversified. Leisurely and with something of an air I strolled along with my heart expanding at the thought that I was a citizen of great Gotham, a sharer in its magnificence and pleasures, a partaker in its glory and prestige.

I turned to cross the street. I heard something buzz like a bee, and then I took a long, pleasant ride with Santos-Dumont.

When I opened my eyes I remembered a smell of gasoline, and I said aloud: "Hasn't it passed yet?"

A hospital nurse laid a hand that was not particularly soft upon my brow that was not at all fevered. A young doctor came along, grinned, and handed me a morning newspaper.

"Want to see how it happened?" he asked cheerily. I read the article. Its headlines began where I heard the buzzing leave off the night before. It closed with these lines:

"—Bellevue Hospital, where it was said that his injuries were not serious. He appeared to be a typical Man About Town."

THE COP AND THE ANTHEM

On his bench in Madison Square Soapy moved uneasily. When wild geese honk high of nights, and when women without sealskin coats grow kind to their husbands, and when Soapy moves uneasily on his bench in the park, you may know that winter is near at hand.

A dead leaf fell in Soapy's lap. That was Jack Frost's card. Jack is kind to the regular denizens of Madison Square, and gives fair warning of his annual call. At the corners of four streets he hands his pasteboard to the North Wind, footman of the mansion of All Outdoors, so that the inhabitants thereof may make ready.

Soapy's mind became cognisant of the fact that the time had come for him to resolve himself into a singular Committee of Ways and Means to provide against the coming rigour. And therefore he moved uneasily on his bench.

The hibernatorial ambitions of Soapy were not of the highest. In them there were no considerations of Mediterranean cruises, of soporific Southern skies drifting in the Vesuvian Bay. Three months on the Island was what his soul craved. Three months of assured board and bed and congenial company, safe from Boreas and bluecoats, seemed to Soapy the essence of things desirable.

For years the hospitable Blackwell's had been his winter quarters. Just as his more fortunate fellow New Yorkers had bought their tickets to Palm Beach and the Riviera each winter, so Soapy had made his humble arrangements for his annual hegira to the Island. And now the time was come. On the previous night three Sabbath newspapers, distributed beneath his coat, about his ankles and over his lap, had failed to repulse the cold as he slept on his bench near the spurting fountain in the ancient square. So the Island loomed big and timely in Soapy's mind. He scorned the provisions made in the name of charity for the city's dependents. In Soapy's opinion the Law was more benign than Philanthropy. There was an endless round of institutions, municipal and eleemosynary, on which he might set out and receive lodging and food accordant with the simple life. But to one of Soapy's proud spirit the gifts of charity are encumbered. If not in coin you must pay in humiliation of spirit for every benefit received at the hands of philanthropy. As Caesar had his Brutus, every bed of charity must have its toll of a bath, every loaf of bread its compensation of a private and personal inquisition. Wherefore it is better to be a guest of the law, which though conducted by rules, does not meddle unduly with a gentleman's private affairs.

Soapy, having decided to go to the Island, at once set about accomplishing his desire. There were many easy ways of doing this. The pleasantest was to dine luxuriously at some expensive restaurant; and then, after declaring insolvency, be handed over quietly and without uproar to a policeman. An accommodating magistrate would do the rest.

Soapy left his bench and strolled out of the square and across the level sea of asphalt, where Broadway and Fifth Avenue flow together. Up Broadway he turned, and halted at a glittering café, where are gathered together nightly the choicest products of the grape, the silkworm and the protoplasm.

Soapy had confidence in himself from the lowest button of his vest upward. He was shaven, and his coat was decent and his neat black, ready-tied four-in-hand had been presented to him by a lady missionary on Thanksgiving Day. If he could reach a table in the restaurant unsuspected success would be his. The portion of him that would show above the table would raise no doubt in the waiter's mind. A roasted mallard duck, thought Soapy, would be about the thing—with a bottle of Chablis, and then Camembert, a demi-tasse and a cigar. One dollar for the cigar would be enough. The total would not be so high as to call forth any supreme manifestation of revenge from the café management; and yet the meat would leave him filled and happy for the journey to his winter refuge.

But as Soapy set foot inside the restaurant door the head waiter's eye fell upon his frayed trousers and decadent shoes. Strong and ready hands turned him about and conveyed him in silence and haste to the sidewalk and averted the ignoble fate of the menaced mallard.

Soapy turned off Broadway. It seemed that his route to the coveted island was not to be an epicurean one. Some other way of entering limbo must be thought of.

At a corner of Sixth Avenue electric lights and cunningly displayed wares behind plate-glass made a shop window conspicuous. Soapy took a cobblestone and dashed it through the glass. People came running around the corner, a policeman in the lead. Soapy stood still, with his hands in his pockets, and smiled at the sight of brass buttons.

"Where's the man that done that?" inquired the officer excitedly.

"Don't you figure out that I might have had something to do with it?" said Soapy, not without sarcasm, but friendly, as one greets good fortune.

The policeman's mind refused to accept Soapy even as a clue. Men who smash windows do not remain to parley with the law's minions. They take to their heels. The policeman saw a man half way down the block running to catch a car. With drawn club he joined in the pursuit. Soapy, with disgust in his heart, loafed along, twice unsuccessful.

On the opposite side of the street was a restaurant of no great pretensions. It catered to large appetites and modest purses. Its crockery and atmosphere were thick; its soup and napery thin. Into this place Soapy took his accusive shoes and telltale trousers without challenge. At a table he sat and consumed beefsteak, flapjacks, doughnuts and pie. And then to the waiter be betrayed the fact that the minutest coin and himself were strangers.

"Now, get busy and call a cop," said Soapy. "And don't keep a gentleman waiting."

"No cop for youse," said the waiter, with a voice like butter cakes and an eye like the cherry in a Manhattan cocktail. "Hey, Con!"

Neatly upon his left ear on the callous pavement two waiters pitched Soapy. He arose, joint by joint, as a carpenter's rule opens, and beat the dust from his clothes. Arrest seemed but a rosy dream. The Island seemed very far away. A policeman who stood before a drug store two doors away laughed and walked down the street.

Five blocks Soapy travelled before his courage permitted him to woo capture again. This time the opportunity presented what he fatuously termed to himself a "cinch." A young woman of a modest and pleasing guise was standing before a show window gazing with sprightly interest at its display of shaving mugs and inkstands, and two yards from the window a large policeman of severe demeanour leaned against a water plug.

It was Soapy's design to assume the role of the despicable and execrated "masher." The refined and elegant appearance of his victim and the contiguity of the conscientious cop encouraged him to believe that he would soon feel the pleasant official clutch upon his arm that would insure his winter quarters on the right little, tight little isle.

Soapy straightened the lady missionary's ready-made tie, dragged his shrinking cuffs into the open, set his hat at a killing cant and sidled toward the young woman. He made eyes at her, was taken with sudden coughs and "hems," smiled, smirked and went brazenly through the impudent and contemptible litany of the "masher." With half an eye Soapy saw that the policeman was watching him fixedly. The young woman moved away a few steps, and again bestowed her absorbed attention upon the shaving mugs. Soapy followed, boldly stepping to her side, raised his hat and said:

"Ah there, Bedelia! Don't you want to come and play in my yard?"

The policeman was still looking. The persecuted young woman had but to beckon a finger and Soapy would be practically en route for his insular haven. Already he imagined he could feel the cozy warmth of the station-house. The young woman faced him and, stretching out a hand, caught Soapy's coat sleeve.

"Sure, Mike," she said joyfully, "if you'll blow me to a pail of suds. I'd have spoke to you sooner, but the cop was watching."

With the young woman playing the clinging ivy to his oak Soapy walked past the policeman overcome with gloom. He seemed doomed to liberty.

At the next corner he shook off his companion and ran. He halted in the district where by night are found the lightest streets, hearts, vows and librettos. Women in furs and men in greatcoats moved gaily in the wintry air. A sudden fear seized Soapy that some dreadful enchantment had rendered him immune to arrest. The thought brought a little of panic upon it, and when he came upon another policeman lounging grandly in front of a transplendent theatre he caught at the immediate straw of "disorderly conduct."

On the sidewalk Soapy began to yell drunken gibberish at the top of his harsh voice. He danced, howled, raved and otherwise disturbed the welkin.

The policeman twirled his club, turned his back to Soapy and remarked to a citizen.

"'Tis one of them Yale lads celebratin' the goose egg they give to the Hartford College. Noisy; but no harm. We've instructions to lave them be."

Disconsolate, Soapy ceased his unavailing racket. Would never a policeman lay hands on him? In his fancy the Island seemed an unattainable Arcadia. He buttoned his thin coat against the chilling wind.

In a cigar store he saw a well-dressed man lighting a cigar at a swinging light. His silk umbrella he had set by the door on entering. Soapy stepped inside, secured the umbrella and sauntered off with it slowly. The man at the cigar light followed hastily.

"My umbrella," he said, sternly.

"Oh, is it?" sneered Soapy, adding insult to petit larceny. "Well, why don't you call a policeman? I took it. Your umbrella! Why don't you call a cop? There stands one on the corner."

The umbrella owner slowed his steps. Soapy did likewise, with a presentiment that luck would again run against him. The policeman looked at the two curiously.

"Of course," said the umbrella man—"that is—well, you know how these mistakes occur—I—if it's your umbrella I hope you'll excuse me—I picked it up this morning in a restaurant—If you recognise it as yours, why—I hope you'll—"

"Of course it's mine," said Soapy, viciously.

The ex-umbrella man retreated. The policeman hurried to assist a tall blonde in an opera cloak across the street in front of a street car that was approaching two blocks away.

Soapy walked eastward through a street damaged by improvements. He hurled the umbrella wrathfully into an excavation. He muttered against the men who wear helmets and carry clubs. Because he wanted to fall into their clutches, they seemed to regard him as a king who could do no wrong.

At length Soapy reached one of the avenues to the east where the glitter and turmoil was but faint. He set his face down this toward Madison Square, for the homing instinct survives even when the home is a park bench.

But on an unusually quiet corner Soapy came to a standstill. Here was an old church, quaint and rambling and gabled. Through one violet-stained window a soft light glowed, where, no doubt, the organist loitered over the keys, making sure of his mastery of the coming Sabbath anthem. For there drifted out to Soapy's ears sweet music that caught and held him transfixed against the convolutions of the iron fence.

The moon was above, lustrous and serene; vehicles and pedestrians were few; sparrows twittered sleepily in the eaves—for a little while the scene might have been a country churchyard. And the anthem that the organist played cemented Soapy to the iron fence, for he had known it well in the days when his life contained such things as mothers and roses and ambitions and friends and immaculate thoughts and collars.

The conjunction of Soapy's receptive state of mind and the influences about the old church wrought a sudden and wonderful change in his soul. He viewed with swift horror the pit into which he had tumbled, the degraded days, unworthy desires, dead hopes, wrecked faculties and base motives that made up his existence.

And also in a moment his heart responded thrillingly to this novel mood. An instantaneous and strong impulse moved him to battle with his desperate fate. He would pull himself out of the mire; he would make a man of himself again; he would conquer the evil that had taken possession of him. There was time; he was comparatively young yet; he would resurrect his old eager ambitions and pursue them without faltering. Those solemn but sweet organ notes had set up a revolution in him. To-morrow he would go into the roaring downtown district and find work. A fur importer had once offered him a place as driver. He would find him to-morrow and ask for the position. He would be somebody in the world. He would—

Soapy felt a hand laid on his arm. He looked quickly around into the broad face of a policeman.

"What are you doin' here?" asked the officer.

"Nothin'," said Soapy.

"Then come along," said the policeman.

"Three months on the Island," said the Magistrate in the Police Court the next morning.

Made in the USA
Coppell, TX
12 September 2021